Sophia Ros
And Came O
The Table, Brushing His Shoulder
To Reach For His Plate.

Her long tresses flowed onto his lap as she brought her face inches from his. He smelled of earth, rawhide and musk, and her breathing quickened as their eyes met. He was a beautiful man who hated her, but right now, she saw desire darken his eyes. She whispered gently, blowing her breath over his lips, playing the vixen he thought she was, "I'll clean this up and then we'll get right to work so you won't have to stay any longer than necessary."

Logan stared at her, their gazes linked and then his hand touched the ribbon of exposed skin at her waist. Her breath caught in her throat and her senses heightened as he splayed his fingers along the rim of her shirt.

It was unexpected magic.

Dear Reader,

I'm beyond thrilled that *Sunset Surrender* is the first book in Harlequin's new Rich, Rugged Ranchers promotion. Rich and rugged (and gorgeous) describes my hero, Logan Slade, to the letter. He owns and operates Sunset Ranch, raising prized horses on land the Slade family has owned for generations.

In *Sunset Surrender,* you'll also meet Sophia Montrose, the beautiful Las Vegas showgirl turned hotel manager who has inherited half of Sunset Lodge located on Slade property. She's a thorn in Logan's backside and a woman who can hold her own against a man who bitterly opposes her return to the ranch. But Sophia isn't the woman he thinks she is—she's more—and she sets out to prove that Logan has always been wrong about her.

Sparks fly between Logan and Sophia and the sizzle is evident from page one. I hope you enjoy seeing Logan's ultimate "surrender" in the first installment of the Slades of Sunset Ranch series. Luke's and Justin's stories are coming soon.

My motto: the bold, passionate, heart-stopping cowboy always gets the girl!

Happy reading!

Charlene Sands

CHARLENE SANDS

SUNSET SURRENDER

H HARLEQUIN®
entertain, enrich, inspire™

Recycling programs
for this product may
not exist in your area.

ISBN-13: 978-0-373-73218-0

SUNSET SURRENDER

Copyright © 2013 by Charlene Swink

This edition published by arrangement with Harlequin Books S.A.

For questions and comments about the quality of this book please contact us
at CustomerService@Harlequin.com.

® and TM are trademarks of Harlequin Enterprises Limited or its corporate
affiliates. Trademarks indicated with ® are registered in the United States Patent
and Trademark Office, the Canadian Trade Marks Office and in other countries.

www.Harlequin.com

Printed in U.S.A.

CHARLENE SANDS

is a *USA TODAY* bestselling author of thirty-five romance novels, writing sexy contemporary romances and stories of the Old West. Her books have been honored with the National Readers Choice Award, the *Cataromance* Reviewer's Choice Award and she's a double recipient of the Booksellers' Best Award. She belongs to the Orange County Chapter and the Los Angeles Chapter of RWA.

Charlene writes bold, passionate, heart-stopping cowboys *and always real good men!* She knows a little something about true romance—she married her high school sweetheart. When not writing, Charlene enjoys sunny Pacific beaches, great coffee, reading books from her favorite authors and spoiling her new baby granddaughters. You can find her on Facebook, Pinterest and Twitter. Charlene loves to hear from her readers. You can write her at P.O. Box 4883, West Hills, CA 91308, or sign up for her newsletter for fun blog posts and ongoing contests at www.charlenesands.com.

With all my love to Everley Frances and Kyra Nicole.
You are my sweet little wonders!

One

Sunset Ranch, Nevada

Sophia Montrose stared into the cowboy's cold black eyes. His mouth was hard and a twitch away from a sneer.

"Couldn't wait to show up here, now could you?"

It was not a sunny welcome back to Sunset Ranch. Not that Sophia really expected one from Logan Slade. She'd decided long ago that she would stand her ground and refuse to let him intimidate her. But she hadn't crossed paths with him since she'd left Sunset Ranch as a girl of fifteen, and had forgotten how his rugged good looks could make her heartbeat speed up. Yet even though maturity had done him justice in a dangerously sinful way, she wouldn't lose sight of how Logan Slade resented her being here, just as much as he had when she'd lived on Slade land before.

"Is Luke home?" Standing on the doorstep of the ranch house, Sophia hoped to see the friendly face of Logan's younger brother soon.

"No. He'll be home tomorrow. You want to come back?"

She shook her head. She had nowhere else to go. She'd given up her small Las Vegas apartment and had driven for hours to reach the ranch this afternoon. She didn't want to take a room in Carson City. She was ready to start her new life, now. This minute. "I came for the keys to the cottage."

He leveled an unforgiving look at her. "You'll get them."

Logan had instructed his attorney not to give her the keys in advance. He'd wanted her to come for them personally. It was Logan's way. He wanted to see her squirm, or at the very least, make her feel uncomfortable the second she stepped foot on Slade property.

She put out her hand, palm up, and tried for civility. "Please. I'd like to get settled."

He assessed her for one moment, then whipped around and entered his house, tossing a command over his shoulder. "Follow me."

She was left on the threshold with her hand out. Quickly lowering it to her side, she tilted her chin up, and took a few steps inside the house.

The minute she entered, her throat tightened and good memories washed away Logan's attempt to ruin this homecoming. The place was as beautiful as she remembered. She'd loved the warmth of the Slade home, the pretty earth colors, the cozily arranged furniture that faced a wide stone fireplace that reached the ceiling. Antiques, bronze statues and expensive artwork decorated the room. Hard wood and contrasting soft hues made the Nevada ranch house perfectly welcoming.

How many times had she played here with Luke? How many birthday parties and private Sunset Lodge events had she attended here with her mother? A stream of good feelings settled into her bones.

She followed behind Logan, his shiny black boots clicking against polished wood. His tall muscular frame ate up space as he sauntered down the long hallway toward his late father

Randall Slade's office. Logan was neat as a pin, looking crisp in a blue plaid shirt and brand-new jeans. Broad-backed and slim-hipped, he had a fine way of filling out his clothes. He made no attempt to speak with her. She didn't expect small talk from him anyway.

Sophia could only imagine his tirade when the terms of his father's last will and testament had been read by the Slades' private attorney. It must have been a last-minute decision on Mr. Slade's part to include her in the will, because when Luke had called—a voice from her past—she'd noted his surprised tone. But he was encouraging. He couldn't wait to see her again after all these years, he'd said, despite the circumstances.

But no one could have been more surprised than Sophia when she'd learned she'd inherited half ownership of Sunset Lodge from Randall Slade. The only stipulation was that she had to manage the lodge for one year before she could sell her share.

It had been twelve years since she'd lived here. Her mother, as the manager of Sunset Lodge, had left abruptly, breaking all ties to the Slade family and asking Sophia to do the same. It meant losing Luke's friendship and many other things, when they'd left Sunset Ranch.

"It's for the best," her mother had said. But Sophia hadn't understood that, the way children couldn't understand sacrifice and hardship and doing the right thing. Sophia had been yanked out of high school in her first year without any warning. She'd left girlfriends behind—and all of her dreams—and had cried herself to sleep every night during those first few months.

Now, with her mother gone after fighting a two-year battle with cancer, Sophia was here to claim her unexpected inheritance. Randall Slade had always been kind to her, showing her compassion, and Sophia thought him a good man. He had treated Sophia like family, had been a father figure to her when her own father had abandoned her at the age of three.

"In here," Logan rasped, ducking into the office.

She followed him inside.

"Have a seat." He pointed to a crimson leather sofa that looked stiff and new. As she gazed around the room, she noted that the entire room had been updated.

Instead of the paneled walls and golden curtains she'd remembered, the walls were clean, textured and stately. Wide electronically controlled windows opened to the grounds outside. Above, rustic chandelier lamps had been replaced with track lights that pointed down at the desk like a row of dutiful soldiers. It was as if all evidence of Randall Slade and his reign at Sunset Ranch had been removed.

"No, thank you." Her decision to stand garnered a quick glance and then a grunt from Logan. Sophia smiled to herself. She'd cling to her small victories.

She wished Luke had been the one to greet her today. She would've liked him to be the first person she'd face upon her return to Sunset Ranch. But she'd moved up her arrival by a few days out of necessity, and maybe it was a good thing to get this confrontation with Logan over with first, rather than hold on to her dread. When she saw Luke again, there wouldn't be worries about his older brother overshadowing their reunion.

"I'm sorry about your father," Sophia said out of reverence to Randall Slade's memory. "He was a decent man. I'm sure you miss him very much."

From behind his long plank desk, Logan's stony expression didn't budge. "We're not here to discuss my relationship with my father."

"You won't even allow me to offer my condolences?" Sophia spoke softly, injured that Logan wouldn't grant her that much. "He was always kind to me."

Leather creaked as he lowered down in a swivel chair behind his desk. "He was kind to Montrose women at the expense of my family."

She stood five feet seven inches tall in bare feet and yet Logan, sitting behind his desk with penetrating eyes locked on her, appeared the more imposing. She swallowed past a lump in her throat. Her mother's death was still painfully raw to her. She knew Logan resented her mother. Maybe he hated her, but she wouldn't allow him to speak ill of her. "My mother died several months ago, Logan. I miss her, just as I'm sure you miss your father. I will ask you to keep your thoughts to yourself about what you think you know."

"I know the truth, Sophia. And there's no way to sugarcoat it." His voice held conviction. "Your mother had an affair with my father, right under my mother's nose. Louisa wanted his money and he was too blinded by her beauty to see what she was doing. Our family was never the same after that. It nearly destroyed us."

Sophia glanced out the window at the beautiful grounds and the stables where exquisite horses were raised to be sold to the highest bidder. The lodge beyond was a private resort designed to house elite guests who wanted a ranch-type experience with all the trimmings.

The Slade brothers—Justin, Luke and Logan—had endured their mother and father's deaths but they had each other, and they'd always have Sunset Ranch, whereas Sophia was completely alone. For whatever pain the Slades went through, she was truly sorry, but what had happened between her mother, Louisa and Randall Slade was complicated and not so easily explained.

"My mother saved your parents' marriage."

Logan shot back, "You've worn too many headdresses in your day, Sophia. All that strutting around half-naked on Las Vegas stages has gotten to you."

His triumphant gaze penetrated straight through her. She shouldn't have been surprised that he knew about her profession as a showgirl. She'd managed to keep under the radar for most of her adult life, but when her mother had taken ill Sophia had tough choices to make to provide for both of them and she wasn't ashamed of it. Nearly everyone within earshot in Nevada had learned about her scandalous marriage to an aging millionaire. What was to be a private union had ended up becoming fodder for the tabloids once the news of her marriage got out. Even in Las Vegas, a twenty-six-year-old showgirl marrying a seventy-one year old oil magnate on the sly was big news.

"So you know?"

"I read, Sophia."

"My marriage and my last profession aren't any of your business," she said softly. Her heart was full of grief and she had no room left for more. Not from Logan and not on her first day back here. There would be more battles to come, she was sure, but she didn't want to argue with him today.

He swept his eyes over her again, this time more precisely, as if he were ranking her on some kind of male scale. He scanned over the long wisps of black hair that had escaped from the severe knot at the back of her head and then his gaze traveled from her amber eyes to her full lips. He lingered there, and she wondered if he remembered the kiss they'd shared in high school. The one that had left Sophia breathless and wanting more. The one that Logan had used to humiliate her. She'd never gotten over her first real kiss or the pain that it had caused her.

"You're beautiful, Sophia," was all seventeen-year-old Logan had had to say as he'd taken her into his arms behind the gymnasium. He'd pressed his body close and kissed her lips as if he were born to do so. It had been glorious and sweet and passionate, all rolled up into one. Sophia had been taken by the sweeping, unexpected feelings stirring around in her belly. On instinct, she had wrapped her arms around his neck and he'd kept on kissing her, Sophia giving in to the older boy's practiced mouth until laughter, from the other side of the brick wall, interrupted them. Logan had abruptly broken off the kiss and stared solemnly into her eyes for a brief moment frozen in time, before he took off, leaving her standing there dumbfounded as he joined his friends.

News of Logan's bet with their three high school classmates—that Sophia wouldn't push him away if he kissed her—had been the buzz all around school the next day. Sophia was easy, just like her mother.

Now she angled her chin down to stare at him, combating the sensations swamping her and wishing she'd never been attracted to Luke's older brother in the first place. She hated that the heat of his gaze did things to her. Hated that she hadn't forgotten that one surprising kiss. It was as if Logan had stamped her for life.

He continued his visual assault with a gaze that traveled along the neckline of her conservative summer dress and lingered on her ample bustline. For as much as she tried, her clothes simply couldn't hide the fullness of her breasts. They were evident no matter what she wore, and she'd actually considered a reduction at one point in her life when putting food on the table and paying hospital bills hadn't yet been a priority. But her body and her exotic Spanish looks had paid the bills when it mattered most. She had to be grateful for that.

Logan's gaze finally scoured over her legs, which were almost in full view from his place behind the desk. She wished she'd sat down when he'd given her the opportunity, rather than be studied this way. Now, under his scrutiny, she tensed.

When he was through eyeing her, he said, "What'd you do, give the old guy heart failure in the bedroom?"

Sophia gasped at the notion and took the comment as an insult, because that's exactly how Logan had intended it. He'd rather think the worst of her than offer her even the slightest ounce of respect. "He's not dead, thank goodness. We're... divorced."

Logan contemplated her for a second. "Short marriage. Was Gordon Gregory smart enough to get a prenup?"

"Not that it's any of your business, but I was the one who demanded it."

Logan leaned back in his chair and laughed. "You don't fool me, Sophia. You're just like your mother."

"Thank you. I'll take that as a compliment. My mother was an amazing woman."

The smile left Logan's face. He came forward in his seat to brace his hands on the desk. Serious now, he stared straight into her eyes. "Look, I'll make you a deal. I'm willing to buy out your half of the lodge. You won't have to stay on and run the place for a year. I can have my attorney get around that stipulation somehow. I'm prepared to make you a mighty generous offer."

"No."

"You don't want to know the amount?" He had a pen in hand, ready to write down a sum.

"No amount of money will do."

Logan didn't seem convinced. He shrugged, and thought she was negotiating. "Let's cut to the chase, Sophia. I'll pay you twice what it's worth."

He took a knife and stabbed her in the heart with that offer. He wanted to get rid of her, and now she knew just how much. But she wouldn't allow that to stop her. She had legal rights to the lodge and no matter what he offered, Sophia wasn't going to leave. "No. I'm staying. I will run Sunset Lodge."

Sunset Ranch had been her home for twelve years. She'd loved living at the cottage next to the lodge. It was the only place she'd ever wanted to live. The only place she'd ever regarded as her home. And she wasn't about to let Logan Slade run her off.

She would stay.

And she would be as successful a manager as her mother had been.

"Now please, Logan. Hand over the keys."

* * *

Logan walked Sophia outside to her car. The old dented Camry looked the worse for wear with nearly bald tires and paint getting thin. The scrap of metal was fifteen years old if it was a day. Hardly the kind of wheels he expected a Las Vegas showgirl who'd been married to a loaded old geezer to drive.

He held on to the cottage keys, wishing his dang father hadn't seen fit to put Sophia in his will. She was too beautiful, too perfect. Every feature on her face was flawless. She had golden eyes, inky black hair and skin that glowed in the Nevada sunshine. She was the kind of woman that made men do stupid things. He didn't want to think about what kind of trouble she would stir up around here. His men would bend over backward for her, he was sure. They'd done the same for Louisa. All that woman had to do was smile pretty, and the ranch hands would do her bidding. She'd had them eating out of the palm of her hand.

Sophia had grown into the spitting image of her mother and then some. In fact, Logan hated to admit it but Sophia Montrose was even more stunning than her mother had been.

"So, refresh my memory. Why in hell do you want to live way out here with the dust and the flies and horse dung?"

Sophia rolled her eyes, and the deep breath she sucked in lifted her ample chest, stretching the material of her dress to its limit. Logan's groin tightened. He didn't like his immediate reaction to her one damn bit.

"Sunset Ranch was my home, too, Logan. For twelve years of my life. It was a happy time, and I loved working alongside my mother at the lodge, which—thanks to your father's kindness—is half mine now. So why would I not want to live here?"

Logan rubbed the back of his neck. He still didn't get why his father put Sophia Montrose in his will. "It's hardly an exciting life."

Sophia repeated his words. "It's hardly an exciting life."

Logan's brows lifted. "You telling me you didn't like living in Las Vegas? A woman like you?"

Sophia narrowed her eyes. "You have no idea who I am, Logan."

He knew she was the kind of woman who wasn't above sleeping with an old man to get her hands on his money. The old codger must have come to his senses before she cleaned him out, prenup or not.

"I can't change the past," she said. "But I'm here to make a life for myself."

"On Slade land."

"Yes, on Slade land. Now, are you going to keep jingling those keys in front of me or are you going to hand them over?"

Logan looked at the keys in his hand. "No one has lived there since you left."

Sophia's brows gathered. "Are you saying that the cottage is exactly the same?"

He nodded. "My father wouldn't allow anyone else to live there. Another victory for Louisa. You can bet that decision didn't set well with my mother. I used to hear them fighting about it late at night."

"That's hardly my mother's fault. Or mine, for that matter."

"You'll have to let the current manager at the lodge go."

Sophia met his smug stare. "Go? What do you mean?"

"I mean, she's out of a job now. The thing of it is, Sophia, you're going to replace her as manager. Last I checked the place can't have two full-time managers. Mrs. Polanski has to be notified."

"You don't honestly expect me to go in there and fire her, do you?"

"Well, if you don't want to, she can stay on and I'll buy you out. That'll solve your problem."

Sophia crossed her arms under her breasts and glared at him. "You go straight to hell."

Logan grinned. He couldn't help it. He'd succeeded in rankling her. Up until this point, she'd been a cool customer. But he'd be darned if the woman didn't just get prettier with her face heating up and her eyes shooting sparks. "I'm just telling you like it is, Sophia. Mrs. Polanski has managed the place going on eight years now. She's good and the guests like her."

"And you left it up to me to fire her. How sweet of you."

"Something has to give. It seems my father didn't think of everything when he gave away our lodge."

"I only have half ownership. He didn't give it all away."

"I bet you wish he had."

She lifted her perfectly sculpted chin and replied without pause. "Yes, sure. I wish I had full ownership."

Logan eyed her. He hadn't expected her to admit it.

"Maybe then I wouldn't have to deal with you…or fire an employee."

Now, Logan's blood boiled. "That lodge has been in the Slade family for generations. It was a little hole-in-the-wall inn for drifters and penniless soldiers after World War II, until my grandfather came along and built it into the fine establishment it is today. You tell me how you figure into that picture?"

Sophia raised her arms into the air, her temper flaring. "I don't know why your father was so generous with me, Logan. I don't know what you want me to say, but obviously your father had faith in me to do the job right. I'm here now and I am going to manage the lodge. If I have to let someone go, I'll do it. But," she said, pointing her finger at his chest, "I can assure you, I will not forget that you placed me in this position the very second I stepped onto the ranch."

"That's the way I want to be remembered, Sophia. As the guy who is going to test you, time and again. You don't belong here, but I won't stand in your way, either, if you do a good job. And don't worry, I'm relinquishing my duties at the lodge to Luke. You'll deal with him from now on." He dropped the keys into her hand. "Starting tomorrow."

She closed her hands around the keys. "I didn't want to start out like this, Logan."

He opened the car door for her and spoke with as much civility as he could muster. "Half a mile down the road. I'm sure you remember how to get there."

"Yes, I do remember," she said. As she squeezed past him to get into the car, her knockout breasts brushed his chest and the firm contact, along with the stirring scent of her erotic perfume, assaulted him like a blow to the gut.

He closed the car door, and watched her Camry vanish into the horizon as half a dozen curses slipped out of his mouth.

The second Logan was out of sight in her rearview mirror, Sophia slumped her shoulders and loosened the tight grip she had on the steering wheel. She eased her foot off the pedal a little and let the car amble along the road that led to Sunset Lodge. She simply would not think of Logan Slade again. He angered her, but he also thrilled her, and it was an emotion she didn't welcome—and one she tried to will away. Her mother had once told her that matters of the heart could not be explained or understood. They just were. Sophia would not be a fool in regard to Logan Slade. He'd offered her a small fortune just to be rid of her. How could she feel anything for him but disdain?

Certainly, she could avoid him while living here. Nestled between the grand Sierra Nevadas and Carson City, Sunset Ranch was vast, spanning miles in a diamond-shaped perimeter. Tomorrow, when Luke arrived home, she'd renew their friendship and she'd deal with him on matters involving her lodge duties. At least she had one friend on Sunset Ranch she could count on.

"Don't you worry about a thing, darlin'," he'd said. "I'll make sure you get a proper welcome home."

Snow from winter storms capped the tallest peaks of the mountain range, reminding her of vanilla ice cream on a waffle cone. The image made her smile. She'd almost forgotten how peaceful and beautiful the landscape was on Sunset Ranch in the spring, the indigo skies dotted with white marshmallow clouds. It was so different from the crowded marquee-laden noisy streets of Las Vegas.

The lodge stables came into view first, and her heart squeezed tight that her mother couldn't be here to see the grounds once again. Louisa had loved caring for the horses in her spare time. "So sorry, Mama."

Sophia blinked away a tear, taking a deep breath.

As she drove a little farther, the lodge filled her vision. It wasn't what one would expect to see on a Nevada ranch. The lodge was grand, made of natural, rounded gray stone mingled with cedar sidings in a glorious combination that spoke of elegance and grace. The surrounding land was fertile and filled with wispy wildflowers in bloom. And the immediate grounds were groomed impeccably.

It was considered a privilege by the employees to tend the property and work the stables. Not too many workers came and went at Sunset Lodge. The Slades had always maintained long-standing relationships with those on staff.

Sophia felt queasy about having to release Mrs. Polanski, and any thought she had of stopping in to see the lodge vanished in an instant. She couldn't face that hurdle right now. She would settle into the cottage first and get organized. She would wait until tomorrow to speak to Luke about the woman.

The cottage was tucked behind and out of view of the lodge. It afforded a good amount of privacy, which Sophia wanted now above all else. The media splash her secret marriage had created, along with watching her mother lose her struggle with cancer, had taken a giant toll on her. She needed to regroup and dive into work she would enjoy. More than anything else, Sophia had to prove something to herself.

All her life, she had gotten by on her looks. She'd never had the chance to go to college, but she'd never regretted the time she'd spent with her mother, helping her manage small motels and inns on the outskirts of Las Vegas. When her mother became ill, Sophia had honed her natural dance abilities to land ensemble roles for big-time casinos in Las Vegas. She'd made enough money to support the two of them as a showgirl, not so much because of her brains or talent, but because she looked the way she did.

Now was her chance to dig in, to give it her all and to shine doing something she loved.

"Ms. Montrose, hello!"

A rider on a gorgeous bay mare sidled up next to the car. She didn't realize how slowly she was actually driving. She rolled the window the rest of the way down.

"It's Ward Halliday. Remember me?"

She glanced at the Slade's head horse wrangler. "Oh, Mr. Halliday. Yes, I do recognize you. How have you been?"

He grinned crookedly. "Getting old and grouchy," he said as he rode along beside her car. "But seeing you here sure brightened my day."

"Well, thank you. It's good be ho—here. I've missed it."

His grin faded and he gave her a solemn nod. "Sure am sorry to hear about your mama, girl."

She put her foot on the brake and the car rolled to a stop. "Thank you. It was a hard time."

"Yeah, I'm sure that it was," he said, pulling up on the mare's reins. "She was a nice woman. She made cookies a time or two for my boy, Hunter. Gosh, he was a little cuss then."

"I remember. I helped her, Mr. Ward."

A sweet smile wrinkled his face. "Heck, you're not fifteen anymore. You can call me Ward. Here comes Hunter now."

He turned in his saddle just as a younger man approached on a horse. "He was just a kid when you left the ranch. He's working here with me now and planning on going to Texas A & M in the fall."

Sophia turned off the engine, and stepped out of the car. The sun beamed down with early afternoon intensity and she shielded her eyes as she gazed up to greet the young man. "So you're little Hunter. It's good to see you again."

He took no offense yet straightened her out good-naturedly. "Not so little anymore, miss."

No, he wasn't. Hunter Halliday was taller than his dad and broader in the shoulders. "I can see that."

"Are you fixin' on moving in right now?" he asked.

"Yes, I was just on my way to the cottage."

Ward looked at the boxes in the backseat of her car. "You need help? Hunter will help you unload."

"Oh, well...I could use a hand, but if you're busy—"

"I'm not busy at all," Hunter said. "Mr. Slade sent me out to see if I can help."

He did? Logan hadn't seemed to care one bit that Sophia had to move all of her things into the cottage by herself. He hadn't offered to help, the way a gentleman would, but then she really hadn't expected much from him. "Then yes. I would appreciate your help."

Ward tipped his hat. "Welcome home, Ms. Montrose."

"Call me Sophia," she said just before he turned his horse around.

"Will do," he called over his shoulder.

Sophia smiled and got back into her car. "I'll meet you at the cottage," she said to Hunter.

Hunter took off and somehow managed to beat her there. He ground-tethered his horse and came forward to open the car door for her.

"You got here fast."

He grinned. "I know a shortcut, miss."

"Of course." She was reminded of all the shortcuts she'd taken on horseback when she lived here. The paved roads weren't always the quickest way from point A to point B. "And please, call me Sophia, too."

He was already reaching into her backseat for a box.

"Sure thing."

He came up with three boxes, stacking them and managing to keep them balanced as he walked to the door. Sophia put the key into the lock. Her heart hammered against her chest, and Hunter beat her to the words that were just forming on her lips.

"I bet it's just the way you remembered it."

She breathed out. "I hope so."

She opened the door without fanfare and moved quietly into the cozy three-bedroom cottage. She glanced around, taking everything in with a quick scan. "It is just as I remembered it."

Hunter glanced around. "I've always wondered what the place looked like on the inside. It's sorta nice. Homey."

"Yes," Sophia agreed. She honestly hadn't known what to expect after Logan informed her no one else had lived here since she and her mother left. Somewhere in the back of her mind, she'd wondered if he would deliberately let the place fall to ruin out of bitterness.

"Where would you like the boxes?" Hunter asked.

She walked into the master bedroom that was once her mother's and forced away her sentimentality for Hunter's sake. She didn't want to cry in front of him. "In here, I think."

He followed her, and then set the boxes on the floor by the long three-drawer dresser. Sunlight streamed inside and cast a golden glow on the room. "Wow, looks like a daisy patch in here."

Sophia smiled. "My mother loved daisies. They were her favorite flower." And the room, decorated with white eyelet curtains covered with teensy daisies and a bedspread of creams and buttercup yellows, depicted that love. "My mama liked things bright. That's how she viewed the world."

Hunter didn't say anything about that. He finished unloading her car and she thanked him for his help. Once she was alone, she sat down on the bed. The curtains were crisp, the bedspread fluffy. There wasn't a speck of dust anywhere. Everything was in good condition—too good to have been left uncared for all this time. Someone had made sure these things were well preserved. And she had a feeling that some-one had been Randall Slade.

He was still taking care of her, even from the grave.

After half an hour of unpacking, the doorbell chimed. It was the same singsong melody that she'd remembered. Cu-rious, she walked to the door and looked through the peep-hole. An older woman stood on the cottage threshold holding a lovely vase of pink roses and greenery.

Sophia opened the door.

"Ms. Montrose?"

She nodded slowly. "Yes, I'm Sophia Montrose."

"I'm Ruth Polanski. I've come to welcome you to Sun-set Lodge."

Sophia shuddered. Ruth Polanski, the manager of the lodge? This was the woman she would have to let go. She wasn't ready for this. She hadn't had time to figure out a way to give the woman the bad news. If Logan sent her over here…

"Would you like to come inside?"

"Just for a minute," the silver-haired woman said. "I'm off duty now and don't want to impose. But I wanted to meet you and give you something to warm your home." She handed Sophia the lovely flower-filled vase. "Welcome," she said, her kind eyes crinkling with her smile.

Sophia held the vase in one hand and gestured for her to enter with the other. Her heart raced. She didn't know if she could do this. And she wondered why Luke hadn't mentioned having to fire an elderly woman in order to take her position as manager. Surely, her friend would have known the delicate position this placed her in. "Thank you. They are beautiful."

"I hope you don't mind me coming over here so quickly.

Hunter stopped by and gave me the news and I was very anxious to meet you. I've managed the lodge for eight years now."

"Oh, uh, yes. Logan informed me of that today."

"I can't tell you how happy I am. I mean, I am sad that Mr. Slade passed on. He was a good man—tough but good—and I promised him something when his heart started failing last year."

"Oh?"

Ruth Polanski stood in the middle of the parlor, looking slightly relieved to be sharing this. "Well, he made me promise to stay on as manager until you came to take over."

"He made you promise to stay?"

"That's right. I've been itching to retire. Everybody on the ranch knows it, too. I've got three grandchildren and a husband who retired last year. But I wouldn't go back on my promise and I never told a soul about our agreement. It's the way he wanted it. Mr. Slade's been good to me, and Logan, well, he's a saint in man's clothing."

Had she been sipping a drink, Sophia would have choked hearing those last words.

"Are you saying you want to quit your position as manager?" Sophia was catching on, and her anger was kicking up steam faster than a whistling tea kettle.

"Why, yes. Didn't Logan tell you? I've been waiting for you to arrive. Of course, I won't leave you high and dry. I'll stick around until you get the hang of our operation here."

"Th-thank you."

"Very welcome. It's not too much different than when you were living here. The lodge still has a great reputation for service and accommodations, and we have the same festivities and trail rides in the spring and summer months that we've always had. I'm sure you know all of this. Whenever you're ready, I'll be happy to show you the ropes. And once I'm gone, Logan will be able to answer any questions you have."

Sophia smiled sweetly. The sainted man would soon get

an earful from her. Sophia wasn't good at playing the victim. She would find a way to get even with Logan Slade for deliberately misleading her. From now on, she would keep her guard up around him. "Yes, Mrs. Polanski, once you're gone, I'm certain Logan will be answering to me."

Two

Morning sunlight beamed in through the daisy-print curtains in a cheerful greeting Sophia wasn't quite ready for. Waking up in her mother's old room, her hazy disorientation didn't last long as her eyes focused and she remembered where she was and that today was the start of her new life. The sun's warmth soaked into her bones and helped soothe away her anger at Logan Slade. Thanks to him, she'd had a hard time falling asleep last night. He'd made sure her homecoming wasn't a thing of dreams. Wouldn't he love to know that Sophia had had her own doubts about moving back here. That she feared that her old surroundings would cause her pain. That maybe she couldn't handle this big a job as well as her mother had. If determination had anything to do with success, then Sophia wouldn't have a worry, because above all else, she would see this through. But doubts still had a way of creeping in after all the mental pep talks faded away.

Six weeks ago, she wouldn't have pictured herself back on Slade land, living at the cottage where she'd grown up and being part owner of glorious Sunset Lodge. The elder Slade and her mother had left this earth just a few months apart and somewhere in the back of her mind, she believed that Louisa and Randall were together now, bonded by love and reunited in spirit. That thought comforted Sophia as she lifted her arms through the sleeves of her flowery silk robe and padded from the soft bedside carpeting onto the stone floor that led to the kitchen.

Sophia had always loved the open-air feel to the kitchen, the large picture window, wood-beam ceilings and textured archways that separated the room from the parlor. The countertops were not built of modern stone, but made with small tiles in varying soft shades of tans and creams. The cabinets were buttercup yellow and the appliances were pristine with analog controls that suited Sophia just fine. She knew every drawer, every cabinet. Everything had been preserved as it once was.

It was too easy to slip back into a time when she'd been happy, when her mother was alive, and when she'd felt free of danger.

A shudder tingled along her spine and thoughts popped into her head of her showgirl days in Las Vegas when she had reason not to feel safe. Just then, she glanced out the window and saw a black-and-white Border collie racing by the cottage. The dog clenched a wooden spatula dripping with something she hoped was lemon batter in his mouth. A dark-haired boy chased him, calling out, "Blackie, come back!"

Sophia chuckled at the scene straight out of a Saturday-morning cartoon. She went to the front door and stepped onto her porch. She spotted the back end of Blackie as he raced around the cottage, tail wagging, seeming to enjoy the sport. The little boy, on the other hand, red-faced from exertion and slowing down, looked ready for the game to end.

Sophia went down the steps and hid behind the front wall, listening for the patter of four paws hitting the ground. Just as the dog turned the corner, Sophia crouched down, surprising the animal. But Blackie was too quick for her. As she lunged, he did a last-second side shuffle and maneuvered away, trotting past her. "Blackie, you stop right now!"

The dog immediately froze, the lemon batter dripping from his mouth, his big brown eyes—dark and innocent—watching her with a curious stare. His little game was over.

The boy rounded the corner next and came to a halt several feet away. His chest heaved up and down rapidly. He had an I'm-not-supposed-to-speak-to-strangers look on his face.

"It's okay," she said softly. "I'm Sophia Montrose. I live here now. I'll be working at Sunset Lodge."

The boy nodded, then shot the dog a quick glance. Blackie had decided to sit his bottom down ten feet away to watch them, with the spatula still clenched between his teeth. Every so often, his tongue would come out to lap up some batter.

"What's your name?" she asked the boy.

He paused for a split second. When he spoke, Sophia knew from the innocence in his voice, he was younger than he appeared. "Edward."

"Hi, Edward. How old are you?"

"T-ten," he said. "H-how—how old are you?"

The boy stuttered, and Sophia hoped it wasn't because she had frightened him in any way. "I'm almost twenty-eight. Looks as if little Blackie has something of yours that you want back."

"Y-yes, ma'am. Only, the s-spatula's not mine. B-Blackie s-stole it from Nana's kitchen at the lodge. And she's gonna be m-mad. He's not s-supposed to go in the k-kitchen."

"I see. Well, I bet that if we talk for a minute and ignore him, Blackie will wander over here, and then we'll get it back."

The boy shifted his gaze to the dog, sunken down to the ground on all fours holding the spatula between his front paws, happily licking away. Edward faced her again with a dubious expression.

"Do you live around here?" she asked.

Shaggy brown hair fell into his eyes when he nodded. "I live with my nana at the l-lodge. She's the c-cook."

Sophia was sure now that she wasn't the cause of the boy's stutter. He seemed comfortable with the fact that the words weren't coming out smoothly, as though his manner of speech was something he'd gotten used to. "Well, then I'm sure I'll be meeting her soon. I'll be starting work at the lodge today."

"Yes, ma'am."

"Is Blackie your dog?"

The boy shook his head. "He belongs to Mr. S-Slade. I feed him and walk him and stuff. It's my j-job."

"I see. Does Blackie belong to Luke or Logan?"

The boy had to think about that a second. "Logan Slade." His dark eyes blinked several times as if a light just dawned inside his head. "You w-won't tell h-him, will you?"

"That Blackie got into the kitchen?"

He nodded.

"No, I won't tell him," she assured him with a smile. "But maybe you should tell your grandmother what happened."

"I l-left the back door open and B-Blackie snuck inside to have b-breakfast with me."

"He did, did he?"

"Nana wasn't there at f-first, but when she came back, she y-yelled at Blackie and that's when he grabbed her s-spatula right outta the b-bowl and took off."

The culprit dog stealing right under Nana's nose made Sophia smile. "I think Blackie likes lemon batter. I can't blame him. I used to sneak a lick or two from the bowl when my mama made lemon chiffon cake."

"Nana lets me l-lick the bowl s-sometimes, too."

The dog finally left the spatula on the ground and trotted

over to Edward. "There, you see," Sophia said. "He came to you."

Edward fluffed the top of the collie's head several times and then lifted his dark-eyed gaze to Sophia. "He's a good dog, u-usually."

"Oh, I can see that he is." Sophia bent down to stroke his rumpled coat and the dog gave her a long grateful look, tongue hanging out. She was no longer the enemy trying to take his treat, but an admirer willing to pet him.

"He's quite a mess," she noted. "I'll get something to wash him down. Wait here."

She walked inside the cottage and seconds later came out with a cloth soaked with hot water. "Go ahead and remove the evidence."

She handed Edward the washcloth, and then strode to where the dog had abandoned the spatula. Bending down, she lifted the dirt-smeared utensil gingerly with two fingers dangling it by the wooden end that was the less filthy. "Your nana might want to retire this one."

"Yes, ma'am." Edward's face crumpled. "She w-won't be h-happy about that."

"I wouldn't think so. Maybe you could make it up to her."

"H-how?"

"There sure are a lot of gorgeous purple wildflowers growing this time of year. Does your nana like flowers?"

He shrugged. "Don't know."

"Most women love flowers. I bet your nana does. A handful of those purple wildflowers and a promise that Blackie won't steal from the kitchen again might make her happy."

The boy pondered that idea with a nod. She set the spatula in his hand and his gaze lingered on her.

"Maybe I'll see you at the lodge later, Edward."

"Okay."

The youngster walked away with the dog at his heels. Just

as Sophia was about to enter the house, he turned around one last time, giving her a long thoughtful stare.

She waved and walked inside.

Sophia showered and picked her clothes carefully for her first day on the job. She'd learned from her mother that the lodge guests wanted the flavor of the Old West, along with their luxuries. Dress professionally, but always keep in mind that this is a ranch establishment. A coral silk dress, cinched at the waist with a wide suede belt, along with a lightweight jacket rolled up at the sleeves and a pair of tan leather boots, gave just the right impression of professional and Western. After dressing, Sophia gobbled up a bowlful of cereal and slurped down coffee, ready and eager to start her day.

She had something to prove.

To Logan Slade.

But mostly to herself.

Half an hour later, Sophia walked into Sunset Lodge. She banked her feelings of nostalgia and disbelief that half of this glorious establishment was actually hers now and crossed the beautifully appointed lobby. Walking past a massive stone fireplace, cozy seating areas and cedar pillars, she turned to the left and headed straight toward the manager's office. She found it in the exact location she'd remembered. The door was open, and she paused for a second at the threshold, her hand fisted and ready for a courtesy knock when Ruth Polanski's voice stopped her in midmotion.

"Welcome, Sophia. Come in, please." Ruth rose from her desk and came forward with a smile. Instead of putting out her hand in greeting, the older woman wrapped both arms around Sophia's shoulders, brought her close and gave her a warm, loving hug. Sophia's heart rang out. She hadn't been held or embraced like this since her mother had passed and now this kindhearted woman—whom she wouldn't have to fire—welcomed her with genuine affection. Sensations of loss enveloped her, making her miss her mother even more.

"Good morning," she said, holding back her emotions.

"I'm glad you're here," Ruth said. "How was your first night back on Sunset Ranch?"

Sophia opted to fib. Ruth didn't need to know how Logan had ruined her sleep last night. "Fine. The cottage is just as I remembered it. I did well."

"Good, my dear. Well, we can get started in here soon enough, but at the moment, I think it's important to show you around the lodge and introduce you to our staff. You may even remember a few of our employees."

"I just might," Sophia said.

"Shall we?"

"That sounds wonderful."

Sophia loved touring the grounds and seeing familiar faces. Many of the employees remembered her as a child and offered condolences regarding her mother. It was a trip down memory lane, but Sophia also focused on what was new, and what might need changing. She'd taken a clipboard with her to jot down notes and when she arrived back in Ruth's office—her office now—she went over the notes with Ruth to get her take on them.

Learning the lodge's new computer system was a breeze. Ruth showed her the basics, and Sophia picked up on it from there. She'd worked alongside her mother at inns and motels for years. There wasn't a program she couldn't figure out. Often her mother had relied on her to navigate new technology.

Poor Ruth. Sophia sensed the woman's eagerness to retire in every anxious glance the lady gave her. When Sophia grasped a new concept easily, the worry lines around the older woman's mouth eased into a small smile. Sophia was all about making a smooth transition and, now that she'd gotten to know Ruth a little better, she was glad that she couldn't foresee any obstacles that would hinder her taking over the reins.

You're not the hired help anymore, Sophia. You own half of the lodge now.

Sophia had a hard time wrapping her mind around that. She'd never owned anything of value in her life. So the transition from employee to owner might just be the hardest of all for her to grasp.

By the end of the day, Ruth bid her goodbye. "These are yours now." She placed a set of keys in Sophia's hand. "You can lock up the office whenever you'd like."

When Sophia blinked her surprise, Ruth shook her head. "I'm not abandoning you, so don't you worry. I'll be here until the end of next week to conclude some business I need to tend to. If you need me to stay on longer, I surely will, but I'm impressed at how quickly you've caught on."

"Thank you," Sophia said. "You've made my first day enjoyable."

"I worked you hard," Ruth said honestly, before her lips lifted gently. "I almost feel guilty about it, but I think you're capable and I'll be sure to tell Logan that."

"You mean, Luke, right? I was told I'll be dealing with Luke from now on."

"Oh, yes, that's right. Though neither one of those boys would ever steer you wrong."

Sophia could argue, but kept her lips buttoned tight.

She walked home in a daze, thinking of what she'd accomplished today, what she was expected to do and how it would all work. Within minutes, she found herself inside the cottage, her boots off, her jacket tossed across the parlor sofa, holding a glass of passion-fruit iced tea in her hand. She plopped onto the sofa, closed her eyes and sipped her tea. When her stomach complained, she remembered she hadn't eaten much today. Excitement mixed with uncertainty had killed her appetite.

She sat in silence and enjoyed the peace but for another growl coming up from the depth of her belly. Then, a few seconds later, she heard a car pull up in front of the cottage. The engine shut off and a door slammed. She rose from her seat so quickly tea splattered onto her dress over her right breast. Wonderful. There was no time to wipe it dry. Her Las Vegas showgirl friends would always tease that she had a natural stop for spillage, and while Sophia had laughed along with them, she'd never really found it too amusing.

She heard footsteps approaching the porch and when the knock came, Sophia was ready, setting her hand on the knob and twisting. She pulled the door open and stared into the incredibly handsome face of a mature Luke Slade.

"Hey, there," he said. "I thought you could use a friend about now."

"So how are you *really* doing, Soph?" Luke asked ten minutes later, after they'd exchanged condolences for the parents they'd lost.

Soph?

He was back to calling her that. Sophia had forgotten how Luke liked to shorten her name. The familiar ring and the slight twang in Luke's voice brought back good memories of the times they'd shared. Any awkwardness Sophia thought that they might encounter in their first meeting never developed. Luke was still Luke. It was a big relief to her to find that the pal she could always rely on hadn't changed too much except to become a confident, gorgeous hunk of a man. She was happy to spend this time with him and Sophia let down her guard to converse with him easily.

Now he sat on the far end of the parlor sofa at an angle facing her, with the heel of one boot resting across his knee, sipping iced tea. He wore faded Wrangler jeans and a blue chambray shirt that was equally faded. His smile and the warmth in his eyes were still the same, though clearly Luke had grown out of his gangly, awkward stage.

"I miss Mama so much, Luke. For so many years it was us against the world. And now that she's gone, I'm a little lost."

"Consider yourself *found,* honey. Sunset Ranch is your home now."

Luke leaned forward and as his work-hardened hands covered hers, she glanced down at their entwined fingers, thankful for his friendship. Luke had always understood her. He'd always had her back. He'd been a good friend, even when they were younger and it wasn't considered cool to have a girl as a friend. Luke had held his own. And as Sophia gave his hand a deliberate squeeze, returning the solace, she waited for a spark to ignite between them. She waited for her palms to sweat. She waited for a tingle.

Seconds ticked by.

Nothing. Not a twinge. No fire.

She'd always wondered whether she'd feel differently about Luke if she were to return to Sunset Ranch. She'd wondered if there would be something more.

She released his hand and lifted her lashes slowly to meet his gaze. Luke had a grin plastered on his face. Clearly he had read her thoughts and had been wondering the same thing. Even though warmth crept up her neck, there was no tension between them. And that was the problem.

"You are a knockout, Sophia, that's for sure."

"You're cowboy eye candy, Luke."

Dubious, he gave a shake of his head, and then each of them threw their heads back and laughed.

Just like when they were kids.

They were friends, period. That much was reestablished and Sophia was glad of that. There was no reason to complicate her life right now anyway. She'd been put through the wringer these past few years, marrying an older man who'd offered to help provide for her mother's medical treatments and praying for a miracle to save her mother's life. She hadn't come out of it unscathed, either. She'd paid a dear price for her high hopes and naïveté.

"Thank you, Luke. You always know how to make me feel better."

He gave her a wink. "Glad to oblige. So what's your game plan?"

"Well," she said, leaning back against the sofa. The chintz material gave underneath her, the cushions fitting her bottom as she curled her legs under her dress and got comfortable. "I hope to make a smooth transition with Ruth Polanski and take over the reins soon. Ruth thinks I'll be ready by the end of next week. I have my doubts." She tilted her head to one side, keeping accusation out of her tone. "And thanks for the heads-up, by the way, buster. You didn't mention that I'd be replacing her as manager."

Luke's beautiful blue eyes rounded innocently. "I didn't think it would be a problem. She's been itching to retire."

"Yes, I found that out the hard way. Your brother led me to believe I'd have to fire Ruth in order to take my position at the lodge."

Luke stared at her for a full five seconds, then rubbed the back of his neck. "Ah, hell."

Sophia let go a heavy sigh.

"Logan was messing with you," Luke said.

"But it wasn't done in jest."

Luke leaned forward to put his glass of tea down on the stone cocktail table. "Don't let him get to you, Sophia. He's got a burr up his butt about what happened in the past. He'll come around soon enough."

"Do you really believe that?" Sophia heard the hope in her own voice. All she wanted to do was live peacefully at Sunset Ranch. She didn't expect Logan to welcome her with open arms, but if he would simply not stand in her way, or better yet, just ignore her, she'd consider it a victory.

Small lines around Luke's eyes crinkled as he winced. "Honestly? Not really. At least not anytime soon. He's more stubborn than I am."

She remembered the arguments she'd had with Luke when they were growing up. He rarely backed down from anything if he thought he had right on his side. "That's saying something," Sophia muttered.

"Hey!"

She smiled. "Just speaking from memory. I'm sure you're more reasonable now."

"Damn straight I am. I mean, I wasn't stubborn so much as I was right and I've always been reasonable."

Sophia nodded, not to belabor the point. It felt good bantering with Luke again.

"So what else did you and my brother talk about yesterday?"

"He tried to…" she began, but then thought better of it.

"Go on." Luke nodded his encouragement. "What did he try to do?"

Sophia didn't want to get between Luke and his brother. There had been enough of that when they were kids. Logan would be rude to her or worse yet, pretend she didn't exist, and Luke would come to her rescue. As a result, the two brothers had been at odds with each other, at least when it had come to her. She didn't want to rekindle that bad blood. "Nothing."

"He did something, Soph. If you don't tell me, I'll go straight to the source. I'll find out."

"Don't bully me, Luke."

"I'm not bullying you, for heaven's sake. But you need to tell me."

Sophia sat silently.

Luke rose slowly from the sofa, battling his reluctance to leave. "All right, I'll go ask my brother if you—"

"Okay, fine. I'll tell you."

He took his seat again.

"You have to promise not to interfere. I don't want to come between the two of you."

Luke's lips tightened and twisted back and forth for so long, Sophia thought he wouldn't agree. "Fine, you have my word."

Sophia took a swallow, sorry now that she'd brought the subject up. "Well, not only did Logan lead me to believe that I'd have to relieve Ruth of her duties, but he tried to buy me out of the inheritance. He said he'd have his lawyer find a way around the stipulation that I stay on for a year to run the place. He offered me a huge sum of money."

"Aw, crap." Luke took to rubbing the back of his neck again. "That guy beats a dead horse, doesn't he?"

Sophia drew back and gasped.

"Sorry. Bad choice of words."

Yes, it was, considering that Sunset Ranch was all about raising and nurturing the finest horses in the country. "He doesn't want me here. Logan's got piss for brains sometimes. He knows damn well he can't buy you out."

"Exactly, but he sure drove his point home about wanting to be rid of me."

"I'm sorrier than you can imagine that I wasn't here to greet you yesterday."

"It's not your fault, Luke. I'll admit that ever since you called me, I've been dying to see you again, but you can't re-schedule *your* life around my comings and goings. I'm a big girl now, and Logan doesn't scare me."

"He may not scare you, Sophia, but he hurt you. And that's just plain wrong if you ask me."

Sophia didn't want the reminder of how Logan had made her feel yesterday. It seemed that for the majority of her life, she'd been on the outside looking in. She'd never gotten over that feeling. That's why coming back to Sunset Ranch, the one place she'd ever felt as though she'd belonged, was so important to her.

"You know what," she said, with a wave of the hand, "let's change the subject. Tell me about yourself, Luke. You mentioned you were in the rodeo for a while. What was that like?"

Sophia settled back and listened to her friend tell her about his life after she'd left Sunset Ranch. And when he offered to take her to dinner for the spiciest chili in the West, her stomach grumbled quietly at the mention of food.

"Yes. I'd love to have dinner with you."

The only thing louder than The Kickin' Kitchen's piped in honky-tonk music was the Red Savina habaneros they put in the chili. The hot stuff made Logan's insides sing like a hillbilly band and required a generous dowsing of cold beer to wash away the flames. After a morning of schmoozing with prospective clients and an afternoon of pencil pushing in his office, he couldn't think of anything better to do tonight than eating a bowlful of chili with a friend.

"You want another go round?" Ward Halliday asked, after slurping up the last spoonful of chili on his plate. Ward had a stomach of iron, which served him well on all-you-can-suffer chili night at Kickin'.

Logan glanced at the empty bowl sitting in front of him. "Nope. I haven't put out the last blaze catching fire in my stomach yet. But you go ahead." He caught the new waitress's eye and crooked his finger.

She sauntered over, giving him a big smile as she approached. "Hi, boys, you ready for more?"

"My friend here will tempt fate once again. You can bring him some," Logan said. "You don't sell antacids for dessert, do you, darlin'?"

She acted as if she hadn't heard that question a thousand times before. As a matter of fact, maybe she hadn't. From what he could recall, being a semiregular and all, the young blonde hadn't worked at Kickin' all that long. Her name tag said she was Shelby from California.

"Hey, not a bad idea. I could start a side business and retire before I'm thirty."

"And what would you do if you retired?" Logan asked, noting how attractive she was in a cute-as-a-button sort of way.

She stared off into the distance for a few beats, before focusing on him with an honest-to-goodness look. "I could tell you what I wouldn't do. I wouldn't be working two jobs and struggling to take care of my grandfather in his tiny house by the interstate. Poor man would have a nice place to live and a real good nurse to care for him in his last days."

"Sorry to hear your grandpa's not well," Logan said.

"I appreciate that. He's a dear man and I'm doing my best." She shrugged a shoulder. "I'm afraid I'm all he's got right now."

Logan eyed the pretty woman with admiration. It was refreshing to hear how loyalty and devotion still meant something to some folks. "Well, then I think he's got a hell of a lot."

The girl's smile returned, beaming on Logan like shining stadium lights. "Thanks, I needed to hear that today. What else can I get for you?"

"You're welcome. And if you could bring us another round of beers, too, I would appreciate it."

"You got it," she said, and turned to take an order from the next table.

Ward shook his head when the waitress was out of earshot. "Man, oh, man."

"What?" Logan didn't wait for Ward to answer before he tipped his head back and guzzled down the remaining drops of his beer.

"You sure know how to sweet-talk a woman."

"That's all it is, is talk, Halliday. Besides, she was real nice." Logan leaned way back in his chair, tipping it on end, stretching out his legs. He hadn't had a date with a woman in a long while. And Shelby from California had piqued his interest enough for him to consider breaking his three-month-long streak of being dateless. But Shelby seemed to have enough on her plate, without dating a man who had no interest in permanence. He chose his women wisely and when he did, it was a just-for-laughs, without-any-strings-attached kind of thing. Whether it lasted one week or a few months, he made sure the women he dated weren't the home-and-hearth kind.

"Well, if Molly could've seen you flirting with that blonde, she would've pestered you until you asked the girl out."

Logan leaned back in his seat. "Your wife's been itching to marry me off."

"Don't I know it? She's forever going on and on about you three Slade boys not getting hitched. I can only imagine the pestering she'll give my boy when Hunter gets of age."

"Hunter doesn't have a girl?"

"No, sir. Right about now, he's focused on attending college in the fall. Saving his money, too."

"That's always a good thing," Logan said. He'd known Hunter since birth, but the big strapping boy wasn't much of a talker. Logan knew he loved horses, though. He'd taken after his father that way. Ward had taught Hunter the value in treating an animal with respect.

A few minutes later, Shelby came by with Ward's second bowl of chili and two more beers. She set everything down on the table. "Here you go, boys."

"Thanks, miss," Ward said, lifting his spoon, ready to dive in.

"You're very welcome," she said, giving Ward her attention before sending Logan another big smile. "If you need anything else, just let me know."

When she turned to help another customer, Logan watched the gentle sway of her hips in her short navy blue waitress uniform.

"Truth is, I haven't had a date in a long while," he muttered.

Ward didn't seem to hear him. He was too busy looking

straight past him and waving his hand with a come-here ges-
ture. Logan craned his head toward Kickin's front door and
a vile curse slipped from his lips.

"Well now, would you look at who's just come in," Ward
was saying. "It's Luke and Ms. Sophia. They're heading this
way."

"Damn it, Ward. Put your hand down, and stop waving
them over."

Baffled by Logan's tone, the older man drew his brows
together. "Why, oh… Oh, right." He shrugged his shoulders
in sheepish apology.

Ward's lightbulb moment was too little too late. The Slades
had always tried to keep their private lives just that—*private*.
But back in the day, news of Louisa Montrose's illicit affair
with his father had leaked out faster than a sledgehammer
to a water pipe, and Logan figured pretty much everyone at
Sunset Ranch knew that he wasn't keen on any of the Montrose women. Especially now. Especially since Randall Slade
had decided to give away half ownership of the lodge to his
mistress's daughter.

Logan hadn't been discreet in his disdain. When he first
heard the news of her inheritance, he slammed his fist into
the barn wall. His damn hand had been bruised for days and,
even though it had healed, every so often the pain would come
back just enough to annoy him.

Very much like Sophia.

Three

Sophia hadn't expected to see Logan in the chili place. She'd been looking forward to sharing the meal with Luke, without any fuss or anxiety. All-you-can-suffer chili sounded like a great plan, but all-you-can-suffer Logan—not so good.

Luke whispered in Sophia's ear as they approached the table. "I swear I didn't know he was going to be here."

"I know," she assured him. In the short time since she'd been reacquainted with Luke, she was sure that he wouldn't have set her up like this.

"We won't stay. Just say hello."

"No, Luke," she said, "I won't have you avoiding your brother because of me."

"Logan won't care if we find another table."

"But I do."

Sophia feared she'd caused a rift between the brothers already. One way or another, she would have to find a way to be civil around Logan, for everyone's sake.

"Hello to both of you," Ward said once they arrived at his

and Logan's booth. "I see you're introducing Ms. Sophia to the fine dining in town."

"I am. Doesn't get finer than Kickin'," Luke said to Ward with a smile, before turning his attention to Logan.

He sipped his beer, and then nodded an acknowledgment to his brother.

She wouldn't allow Logan to ignore her and opted to be the bigger person. "It's good to see you again, Ward. And you, too, Logan."

Logan slanted a look her way, his gaze landing on the bodice of her coral dress. He refused to make eye contact with her, as if she wasn't worthy of any more of his attention than that. "Sophia."

Idiot.

"I'm having me a second bowl of Number Three," Ward said, in an attempt to ease the tension at the table. "The higher the number, the higher the heat level. Only goes up to five. But I'm not that brave."

"I think three's pretty brave," Sophia said. Kickin' Kitchen wasn't around when she lived here, and now her interest was piqued. Her Spanish ancestry and mother's heavy hand with spices gave her a taste for daring foods.

"Beginner's start at Number One and pretty much stay there for a few years," Logan said smugly, eyeing her with a challenge in his eyes. "Some can't even handle that."

Sophia straightened to her full height. Mr. High and Mighty actually volunteered something more than a grunt. She shot her chin out, and took the bait. But she planned for him to be the one eating crow. "I bet I could handle Number Three."

Logan stopped drinking his beer long enough to say, "That I'd like to see."

"Whoa, Sophia," Luke said with a shake of the head. "I just graduated to Three a few months ago."

Ward gave her a skeptical look.

Sophia took Logan's challenge. "I'd be happy to prove you wrong."

The waitress came sprinting by to deliver a round of drinks to the booth. "You folks need a table?" she asked Luke. "'Cause we're getting slammed. It's a twenty-minute wait."

"That's fine. We'll wait," Luke said with a firm nod, clearly protecting Sophia. "Slade. Table for two."

Logan set his beer bottle down with a thud and his dark eyes sharpened on her. "Chickening out?"

Luke shook his head at Sophia, his eyes darkening with caution, but it was too late for his warning. Her mind was made up. For one, she wouldn't let Luke baby her and, two, Logan needed to be put in his place. When Ward rose to offer her a seat, she lowered down and slid across the booth, making room for him to sit beside her.

"I'm not chickening out," she said triumphantly to Logan, and then turned to flash Ward a generous smile. "Thank you, kind sir."

Ward nodded, color rising up on his neck. "Welcome."

Logan's mouth twitched, and he sighed with resignation as he made room for his brother in the booth. "Yeah, sure. Why not."

"Cancel that table for two," Luke said to the waitress as he took a seat beside Logan. "Looks like we'll be joining them."

"Sure thing. I'll be back in a sec with menus."

Before the waitress turned away, Luke stopped her with a gentle command. "No need. We know what we want." Luke met with Sophia's eyes once again. She nodded, giving the waitress her order. "I'll have a Number Three."

"Make that two Number Threes," Luke said with a sigh, "and two beers."

"No beer for me," Sophia said. "I'll have water."

The waitress made a mental note.

"You'd best bring three glasses of ice water then, for starters," Ward said, looking a bit concerned. "Those habaneros will drain the last ounce of moisture from your mouth."

"Sure, I'll be back with waters, beer and two Number Threes." The waitress moved on and Sophia found herself facing Logan directly across the booth.

It wasn't a hard picture, seeing the two Slade cowboys sitting side by side. They had similar good looks. The biggest difference was that Luke's eyes were blue, like his mother's, and his hair was a sandy color, rather than Logan's dark brown. But the men were worlds apart in personality traits.

Luke inclined his head toward Sophia. "Beer might have quenched your thirst better."

"I don't drink."

"Ever?" Luke asked, looking a little astonished. "I'm sorry. I didn't know."

"You couldn't possibly know," she said quietly, holding in her anguish. Luke didn't know everything there was to know about the grown-up woman she'd become, unlike Logan, who *thought* he knew everything about her. "My father was an alcoholic," she explained, "and I've never found a taste for the stuff. It's my way of rebelling."

Not that she felt obligated to give a reason, but her father's story was a constant reminder of the pitfalls and fragile nature of the human spirit and she especially wanted Logan to understand that her life hadn't been all peaches and cream. His family didn't have a monopoly on heartache. Despite being married to a loving beautiful woman, Sophia's father had left her mother with a three-year-old child to raise. As an adult it was still pretty hard for her to rationalize his actions, though she'd tried hard to work through being fatherless most of her life. Alberto Montrose chose a love affair with liquor that ultimately ruined him. The last Sophia had heard, which was more than ten years ago, her father had been seen wandering the streets of San Francisco, ragged and homeless. Liquor *was* his wife, child, addiction and downfall, all rolled up into one.

"Enough said," Luke announced, wearing a compassionate expression. "Water is underrated anyway."

"Yeah, you can't live without it," Ward offered needlessly.

Logan chuckled, and sipped his beer, watching her as if she were a spectacle. "Your stomach's gonna rebel in a few minutes."

This time Luke wasn't disagreeing. "You're in for it, Sophia. But you always were a daredevil. That much I do know."

"Me? What about wrestling bucking broncos for five years of your life?"

"Six," Ward and Luke said in unison.

"And I wasn't wrestling with them, darlin'. I rode them for nine seconds at a time."

"Most times, it was five seconds in the saddle, and the rest of the time on the ground, eating the horse's dust," Logan offered, happy to give Luke a bad time.

"Eating dust may be easier than eating Number Threes."

Sophia gave the men an eye-roll and shook her head. "I will consider myself properly warned by all three of you. I promise you I'll hold my own."

She moved her long hair to one shoulder and shuffled in her seat, adjusting to the booth's cushion to get more comfortable. Logan watched her movements, his gaze flicking over her body until their eyes finally met in a daring stare. A hot sprinkle of desire spread through her belly like warm sugar. For the slightest pinch of time, Sophia spotted a glimmer of admiration in his eyes for what she was about to do. Which, in her estimation, wasn't all that admirable. She would eat a bowl of Kickin' chili. How hard would that be?

And in that moment, no matter how much she hated to admit it, she saw Logan in a different light. She saw him as someone who could match her spirit, someone she might enjoy being around and someone who could fill the gaping void threatening to swallow her up. A shell that no one, not even a wonderful man like Luke, could ever fill.

"What the hell?" Ward jerked in his seat and all heads turned his way. "Pardon me, miss." Apology touched his eyes as he briefly glanced at her, before pulling his cell phone out of his pocket. "Darn vibrating thing. Always shocks the vinegar outta me."

Logan's short laugh flashed a smile that cut deep ridges into each side of his mouth. Sophia took a quick breath and focused on Ward rather than allow that warm-sugar sensation to spread any further. She reminded herself that Logan hated her.

Ward glanced at the phone's screen. "It's a call from Hunter. He wouldn't be calling if it weren't important."

Logan said, "Go ahead and answer it, Ward."

Ward spoke to his son, nodding his head and saying "uh-huh, uh-huh," about half a dozen times. He finished his conversation with, "Okay, I'll be right there."

Ward set the phone back into his pocket as he spoke. "My boy needs help at the ranch. Skylar is foaling early. He's thinking it's gonna be a difficult delivery. Luke, she's your favorite mare. You coming with me?"

Ward rose from his seat. Luke did, too, blinking away the fear on his face. "Yeah, I'd better see to her."

From what Sophia gathered, no one on the ranch knew more about horses than Luke. He had a natural way with them. Even Ward, Sunset Ranch's head wrangler, seemed to look to Luke for help.

"Sorry, Soph. I've got to go. We almost lost her last time she foaled."

"Okay, I understand," Sophia said, grabbing her clutch purse, "I'll go with you."

"No," Luke said. "You stay and eat your dinner. I know you're hungry. Your meal is coming."

"But I, uh—" Sophia looked from Logan's unreadable expression to Luke. "I don't have to—"

"For Pete's sake, woman," Logan said with a shake of the

head. "I won't bite. Ward can drive to the ranch with Luke. I'll take you home later. After you eat your Number Three."

"But—"

"Are you chickening out again?"

"No!"

"Okay, then." Logan slid his brother a reassuring look. "You go on. Don't worry about anything but saving Skylar and her foal."

"Play nice," Luke said, pointing his finger at Logan.

"Get outta here," Logan said, grabbing for his beer with a casual shrug, as if to say he didn't have anything to worry about.

Luke didn't budge. "Logan."

"Damn it, you have my word."

Finally satisfied, Luke nodded. "Fair enough. I'm sorry, Sophia," Luke said. "But Logan will get you home safely. I've really gotta run."

Ward had already excused himself and was waiting for Luke by the entranceway. "I'll be fine. Don't worry about me. I only hope it goes well for the mare." Luke met up with Ward and the two men exited the café in a hurry. And just like that, Sophia found herself alone with Logan Slade.

He was stuck with Sophia for the rest of the night. Hell, a man could do much worse than entertaining a gorgeous woman with a killer body for the evening. She was a damn sight better to look at than the antique cast-iron pots and pans hanging on the wall. A damn sight more appealing than rusted tricycles and red wagons that littered the shelves circling the perimeter of the café. She sure had every man in the joint giving her the eye and giving him a solid way-to-go look as they scanned the booth. Logan would be on his best behavior tonight. Not because he'd eased up on his thinking about Sophia, but because he'd given his brother his word. For Luke's sake, Logan would treat Sophia kindly.

After a long minute of silence, she asked, "Do you think the mare will be okay?"

He blew out a breath. "Don't know. Birthing can be tricky at times. Skylar is a trouper though. She's strong and if anyone can help her, it'd be Luke."

"That's what I've heard. Luke knows a lot about horses."

"He does," Logan said, keeping his tone light. If the woman wanted to praise his brother to high heaven tonight, he wouldn't stop her. He wouldn't like it much, but he wouldn't stop her. The two of them were already thick as thieves again.

His brother's relationship with Sophia had always irked him. Logan was the oldest of the three boys—Justin being the youngest. Logan had been very close to Luke until Sophia had gotten in the way. Ever since their friendship had developed, Logan felt like he'd been left out in the cold. Montrose women had managed to shred Slade family loyalty. It shouldn't be so, but Luke couldn't see it any more than his father had. Their blindness left a bitter taste in Logan's mouth, sharper than the chili he'd just polished off. His only consolation was that Shelby was heading toward the table with Sophia's burn-as-it-goes-down chili on her tray. "Your chili's coming up."

The waitress set the bowl in front of Sophia. Spicy aromatic scents of peppers, onions and cilantro drifted to his side of the table. "Thanks, Shelby."

"You got it." She shot him another sweet smile before walking away.

Sophia took her time, opening her cloth napkin and placing it on her lap. Then she lifted her lashes and those brilliant amber eyes surrounded with flecks of gold fell on him. "Smells delicious," she said.

"That's why we're here."

The second he said "we," his pulse pounded in his ears and images popped into his head of the two of them, really playing nice. For anyone in the café watching, it might appear that they were on a date.

It'd be a cold day in hell, he thought, yet he couldn't take his eyes off her.

Sophia dipped into the chili and came up with a rounded spoonful with cheese dripping off the sides. Steam shot straight up for half a yard then disappeared into the air. Sophia pursed her lips and blew gently, her mouth forming a small *O* to whisper away the heat.

Logan's Adam's apple bobbed in his throat. His damn body pinched tight, and he sat mesmerized as Sophia prepared to take her first bite of ass-kicking chili. Logan had never thought of chili and sex together, but now, that's all he could think about. Watching her take her first bite, swallow, then gaze up at him, looking satisfied and accomplished, gave him a sexual thrill that he'd never experienced before. It was beyond crazy and like a fool, he grinned.

So did she.

The light in her eyes matched the way he was feeling inside, most likely for entirely different reasons. "Piece of cake," she said.

Piece of something, he thought, grateful the lower half of him was covered by the table. It hadn't escaped him that *he* was the one suffering as Sophia ate from her bowl of all-you-can-suffer Kickin' chili.

He watched her eat three more spoonfuls without even a slight flinch. The woman was good at spicy.

"You know," she began, stirring the chili with the stainless-steel spoon, "it was nice of you to ask Hunter to help me move in yesterday."

"Who said I asked him?" he shot back.

"So you didn't?" Her almond-shaped eyes rounded in surprise.

He shrugged. "Maybe I did."

"I didn't think you'd given it a thought. You didn't personally offer to help."

"Did you expect me to?"

"I had hoped you'd be a gentleman. I didn't want to start off at Sunset Ranch with bad feelings."

Logan ignored that last part of her statement. He wasn't in the mood to get into it with her tonight. "I'm not the welcoming committee. I have a ranch to run. Hunter helped you. Isn't that good enough?"

"Yes, I suppose. I was beginning to feel good about that, and you, until you set me up with Ruth Polanski. It was a low blow, even coming from you, Logan. You led me to believe I had to fire the woman."

Logan scrubbed his jaw. It wasn't his proudest moment, but he'd been angry and wanted to lash out at her when she'd first arrived. She'd called it correctly. It had been a low blow. Logan didn't play dirty. Not usually. Yet he wasn't ready to apologize. "You must have been pleasantly surprised when you learned you didn't have to let her go."

"I worried about it all night."

He put himself in a no-guilt zone and hung tight. "I'm sure you slept well enough."

Sophia shook her head and her long wavy hair, caressing one side of her shoulder, flowed over her breast. "You need to let go of the past, Logan. You'd be a happier man."

A lecture, coming from her? "What makes you think I'm not happy? I'm sitting here, watching you pretend to stomach that chili. Tell the truth, Sophia. It's burning like hell now."

To his surprise, she put her hand just under her breasts, spread her fingers out over her stomach and delivered a low rumble of laughter. "You'd love to believe that."

"You won't admit it?"

"Maybe it's more fun to keep you guessing. When's the last time you've had fun, Logan?"

"What do you care?"

"That long?" Sophia asked, shaking her head as she lifted another spoonful to her mouth.

The woman was getting to him and damn if he wasn't enjoying himself. Not because he thought Sophia was suffering with the chili, but because she was a woman who stood up to a challenge and managed to keep him guessing.

"You're forgetting who's driving you home."

"Oh, no. I am very well aware," she said, her amber eyes blazing with warmth enough to make heat crawl up his belly *and* put a lump in his throat.

He swigged the last ounce of his beer with a quick gulp.

Sophia, on the other hand, had yet to reach for her glass of water.

Sophia sank into the comfy, forgiving seat cushion of Logan's black pickup truck. The luxury four-wheel drive sported a polished wood and beige leather interior with a dashboard full of digital controls an airline pilot would envy. She fastened her seat belt and watched the scenery go by as they exited the café's parking lot and took to the open road. An hour ago, the golden sunset had faded and now lights from the town they left behind sparkled like tiny diamonds in her side rearview mirror.

Sophia eyed Logan as he drove with one hand on top of the steering wheel. Country music played softly. The lack of conversation was actually comforting. They'd extinguished their small talk while in the café. She couldn't think of anything else she wanted to say to him that didn't involve business, and Sophia wasn't in the mood to spar with him about that right now.

Logan was used to comfort, style and the finer things in life. Even though he lived on a ranch, everything he owned, from his classic felt Stetson hat and expensive tooled-leather boots to the exquisite sprawling ranch home, was top-notch. She hadn't missed the one-hundred-dollar tip he'd laid on the table for the waitress just minutes ago. She had gushed and tried to give it back, but Logan had insisted on her keeping it. Apparently, he had money to burn. Sophia would bet her last dollar that the designer watch he wore on his wrist cost more than her mother's yearly salary when she'd worked at the Desert Breeze Motor Inn.

They'd spent three years working in that dive, before Louisa had finally landed a job more suitable for her managerial skills. In many respects though, the life Sophia had with her mother was richer and worth more than any of the material possessions she could ever hope to own.

Sophia had gotten a small taste of the good life when she'd married. Though many believed she'd married the older man for his money, Sophia had convinced her mother that she'd married for the promise of love. When in truth, neither had been true *exactly*.

A sharp jolting pain twitched in her stomach. She gasped silently, holding her hands firmly in place when her initial reaction was to rub her belly. The pain was fleeting, and then it was gone. Sophia released the breath caught in her throat. She'd be okay. The chili had gone down smoothly earlier and at the time, she hadn't had any doubts about it.

Another jolt hit her. This time, the pain spiraled up, burning toward her rib cage. "Oh," she breathed out as slowly and as quietly as she could, slanting a look at Logan, who was listening to the country music playing on the radio, his focus on the dark road ahead.

The next pang hit and her body tightened up. She grabbed her clutch purse and set it onto her stomach, then slid her hand underneath it. Her fingers dug in and she tried to smooth away the rebellion going on inside.

"Ohh." The pain gripped her hard this time and she leaned forward and hugged her stomach with both arms. Beads of sweat moistened her forehead.

Logan shot a glance at her. "It finally hit you?"

She bit her lip and nodded helplessly.

"Is it bad?"

Again, she nodded. Perspiration trickled down the back of her neck, sticking to her hair.

"Hang on. I'll get you home fast."

Logan revved the engine and the truck roared down the highway. Minutes later they reached the gates of Sunset Ranch and Logan slowed the truck. "My house or the cottage?"

"Take me home," she said, wanting the comfort of her own surroundings, new as they were, but also familiar.

The truck roared to life again and after a short time, the dimmed lamppost lights in front of the stone house came into view. Sophia thanked all things holy that she was finally home.

Logan brought the truck to an abrupt halt. He got out, and she heard his boots on the gravel path as he approached the passenger's side. Doubled over now, she pressed both arms against her belly, attempting to make the aching go away. Logan opened her door and when their eyes met, the stern set of his jaw softened and he cursed. "I'll get you out."

Before she could protest, he bent down to unfasten her seat belt, removing her arms from around her belly first to get them out of his way.

"It's not necessary to carry me," she whispered.

Her statement fell on deaf ears. He scooped her from the seat, one hand lifting under her knees, the other at her shoulders. As if this weren't humiliating enough, her dress slid to her upper thighs. Logan's gaze locked onto her legs shamelessly as he brought her out of the truck. His hip shoved the door closed.

As he strode purposefully toward her front door, Sophia clung to his neck, giving in to the power and strength of his arms. Cradled this way, she felt safe and protected, though she knew in her head she should be wary of him. She shouldn't let down her guard. Once they reached the porch, he set her legs down, reached into his pocket and came out with a set of keys. He inserted one into the lock and kicked open the front door. Then he picked her back up.

Moonlight streamed inside, illuminating the front room just enough to guide the way. Logan moved with the grace of a cat into the house, finding the parlor sofa easily. He lowered her gently onto her backside. With her arms still locked around his neck, Logan's face came within inches of hers and their gazes met through the darkness. A brief moment passed between them. The dark coolness in his eyes blazed now with heat so strong, memories flooded Sophia's mind of the one blissful, wonderful, sizzling kiss they'd shared so long ago. Her stomach stopped aching for a short time and she became mesmerized by the possibility that was Logan Slade. But just as her mind wrapped around the idea, the heat in Logan's eyes offering that possibility died away, replaced again by a cold, unreadable stare. Sophia swallowed hard, relinquishing the moment to foolishness.

Logan unlocked her arms from around his neck and rose to full height. "I'll be right back."

She lay her head down on the arm of the sofa and listened as he went to his truck. When he returned, he flipped on a lamp on the end table. Soft light flowed into the room. Standing over her, he lifted her hand in his and plopped two round pink tablets down in her palm. "Take these first," he said.

She stared at them.

"They will help," he offered, his voice gruff.

They might be poison for all she knew, but she was pretty sure they were antacids, and though she was certain they wouldn't help, she lifted them to her lips, opened her mouth and chewed. They went down like chalk and made her mouth dry.

"Now," Logan said, "Take a swig of this."

He bent onto his knees by the sofa. With a gentle hand, he lifted her head and guided a pink bottle to her lips.

She shook her head. Mixing medications wasn't wise. "I don't think so."

He leaned back a little, holding the bottle away from her. "Trust me on this, it works. I've been where you are now. Why do you suppose I carry this stuff in my truck on Kickin' days?"

Sophia closed her eyes to the look of concern on Logan's face. It didn't make sense that he would try to help her. He detested her and wanted her gone *yesterday*. How could she trust him?

Another cutting pain seized her stomach. "Oh."

His hand, still nestled in her hair, lifted her head up a little more. "C'mon, Sophia. Just drink it."

She bit the bullet and gave him her trust, craning her neck forward. He tipped the bottle, and she sipped from it a few times.

"That's good," he said. "Give it a few minutes."

She lay her head down after swallowing the awful liquid. "You don't have to stay."

Once again, he ignored her comment. He rose and walked off. She listened for the front door to close, hoping that he'd leave, but instead she heard him fidgeting around in the kitchen. He turned on the microwave. The thought of food of any sort made her queasy.

Her eyes drifted closed and only when she felt something warm being placed on her belly, did she open them again. The warmed dishtowel acted much like a heating pad and soon, between the meds and the heat, the gripping pain in her stomach began to ease.

"You should take a warm bath later," he said.

She lifted her gaze to Logan's face.

"Of course, I'd offer to do that with you, too," he said, the momentary flicker of heat once again in his eyes, "but I've got a feeling that wouldn't go over too well."

It hurt to smile, but Sophia managed to anyway. "You'll never know."

"The way I didn't know you were going to be sick?"

Humiliation mixed with anger and Sophia hinged her body forward to get up from the sofa. "Is that why you're here? To rub my nose in it?"

He laid a hand on her shoulder, easing her back down. "Lay back. Don't get riled."

"Don't rile me then." Her head plopped down on the arm of the sofa again.

"You don't like being wrong."

"Why are you helping me?" She turned her head to face him.

"You don't know my compassionate side."

"Do you have one?"

"Are you feeling better yet?"

Sophia stopped arguing with Logan long enough to realize she was feeling better. Almost as quickly as her stomach had become unsettled, it began to feel remarkably normal again. "Yes, I am." She glanced into his eyes. They were so intense and stubborn one minute, and then so kind and caring the next. "I do feel better."

Logan nodded. "I don't kick a person when they're down."

"You mean you want a level playing field for when you destroy me?"

"I never said I wanted to destroy you, *Soph*."

Soph?

And then it all became clear. Just when she'd thought Logan might have come around and wanted to be civil to her, just when she thought the past was forgiven and they could start anew, she caught on to what he was doing. She still owed him her thanks for helping her recover from her suffering tonight, but now she knew the reason why. "It's because of Luke, isn't it? You promised to see me home safely and you're a man of your word. You're doing this for Luke. Not for me."

His eyebrows dented into his forehead. "You have a strange way of thanking a man."

Sophia's ire sparked. Logan ran hot and cold with her and she never knew where she stood with him. Her frustration echoed in a shrewish raised voice. "How would you like me to thank you?"

Instantly, his gaze swept over her as she lay on the couch. "Let me give you that bath and we can call it even."

The idea of bathing with Logan brought a different kind of queasiness to her belly. Images danced in her head. But she was weak where Logan Slade was concerned. He didn't deserve her passionate thoughts.

But then another thought entered her mind, an uncomfortable memory that had nothing to do with Logan at all. *Don't go there, Sophia,* she reminded herself. You don't have to be afraid anymore. But the image from her Las Vegas days wouldn't leave her.

She had been sitting in front of her dressing-room mirror backstage before her performance when she discovered the first note tucked under her makeup case. Bone-chilling fear had traveled along her spine when she read the words.

You are too beautiful, Sophia. You will be mine one day.

She'd received five similar notes, all with the same strange sentiment. What had freaked her out the most was that the person sending the notes had known a lot about her. She'd found envelopes printed with her name on the front windshield of her car or left for her at the motel where her mother worked. The actual words weren't threatening, so she'd never gone to the police, and she'd never worried her mother about them, either. But Sophia had been frightened on more than one occasion when she'd sensed that someone had been watching her.

After a while, Sophia started really looking at the faces of the men who would come to her shows. She began wondering if the note writer was among them, studying her.

"Thinking about it?" Logan asked, taunting her to answer.

Sophia returned her attention to the man who had rescued her this evening, the man who had invited himself to bathe with her. He had known what her answer would be before he suggested it. He wasn't serious. Perhaps, if she had an inkling that he was, she might be persuaded to change her mind. *Yes, join me in a bath, Logan.*

But Sophia was through playing his games tonight. She had enough bad memories to battle and now a queasy stomach to deal with. He'd been kind earlier and she'd wanted to believe that they could get along. She'd relished being in his arms while he carried her inside. She'd appreciated him staying to make sure she would recover. But had she only imagined his concern?

"You should go now."

He looked at her sprawled out on the sofa and inhaled sharply, as if the idea of bathing with her hadn't been a joke. "Yeah, I was thinking that same thing."

"Th-thank you for driving me home," she said through tight lips that didn't want to form the words. "And for...for helping me tonight."

He gave her a quick nod.

Sophia turned away from him then, feeling mixed up inside. She closed her eyes to the sound of Logan's footsteps fading away. There was no fond farewell from him. No "I hope you feel better," and no "Call me if you need my help again." It was a chilling reminder for her not to let down her guard with Logan. He would fool her time and time again, if she allowed it.

The front door opened and closed, and then he was gone.

Only then did Sophia realize that Logan Slade had his own key to the cottage.

He could barge in on her anytime he wanted.

Four

Constance Branford offered Sophia a lemon poppy seed muffin with strawberry filling. She'd briefly met the lodge's head cook yesterday on her tour with Ruth, and now Sophia sat beside her at a long country oak table, the only piece of furniture in the lodge's spotless stainless-steel kitchen that wasn't updated and brand-new. "Oh, no thanks, Constance. I couldn't possibly."

Edward's nana withdrew the basket. To avoid insulting the chef, Sophia quickly explained, "I had my first encounter with Kickin's chili last night. My stomach is still touchy."

Constance made a tsking sound. "That's not food," she said with a shake of her head. "I don't know why the men go there. Edward's been hounding me to let him eat there, but it's not for a young one's stomach. He'll just have to wait."

Sophia smiled. The head chef certainly had her ideas about what constituted a good meal. "Apparently, it's not for my stomach, either. I should stick to the lodge's food." She took in the broad range of pastries, biscuits and muffins set out and ready to be served. Behind them, two sous chefs were busy chopping up vegetables and preparing batters. She thought about how Blackie had made off with the spatula right under Constance's nose and how Edward had offered her his apology. The boy had taken Sophia's advice. Right in the middle of the table in a clear mason jar sat a small bouquet of wildflowers, picked straight from the fields outside the lodge.

"Your grandson is a nice boy," Sophia said.

"He's mischievous, like any ten-year-old, but yes, a good boy. He's had a rough time without his parents." Constance, whose eyes brightened when speaking of Edward, didn't fit the mold of a white-haired, rocking-chair nana at all. The astute, intelligent woman who ran the lodge's kitchen was quite capable, but there was an underlying current of sadness in her expression, too.

"I know something about losing a parent. It's never easy, but with a child…"

Constance shook her head. "Edward's parents aren't dead."

Sophia blinked.

"My son and his wife have drug addictions. It got really bad and the first seven years of Edward's life were tumultuous. They left Edward with me, and I have legal custody."

"Oh. I'm sorry to hear that." Sophia had experience with her father's addiction but poor Edward had to live through that turmoil with both of his parents. At least for Sophia, she'd been blessed with a loving mother to raise her, but the boy hadn't been so lucky. Perhaps the resulting trauma was responsible for his speech problems.

"The best thing those two ever did was to hand over his custody to me without putting up a fight. They knew Edward would be better off with me. I'm doing the best I can to give him a stable home."

"Sunset Ranch is the best place for that. I grew up on the ranch and loved living here as a child."

"I agree. And Logan has been kind to Edward, giving

him responsibilities on the ranch to make my grandson feel needed. Letting him take care of Blackie was a very good idea."

Logan again? Why did everyone think the man a saint? But in this case, Sophia couldn't begrudge his kindness to the boy. "Boys and dogs go hand in hand."

Constance glanced at her watch. "He should be back from walking the dog soon. He gets up early on school days to feed and walk Blackie."

"Shall we go over this month's menus now, before he gets here?"

"Certainly. Can you handle coffee?"

"It smells delicious." She stroked her tender stomach that was begging for something warm and comforting. "I would love some."

Constance poured them both a cup and they got down to business. Sophia had some ideas for a summery theme for next month's menu. But she had to be delicate about making suggestions. Stepping into Ruth's shoes, and trying to make changes this early on, could ruffle feathers. Even so, Sophia was determined to have a hand in everything going on at Sunset Ranch. She remembered her mother's prowess and how involved she'd been with every aspect of the lodge.

Ten minutes later after a productive conversation with Constance, Edward walked through the kitchen doors, wearing a backpack and a shy smile. Sophia waved at him as he shuffled his way over to his nana.

"Edward," Constance said, "have you fed and walked Blackie already?"

He nodded and slipped Sophia a guilty glance. She reassured him with a friendly smile that said their little secret was safe, not that she'd ever tattle on the boy to Logan about their encounter yesterday, or anything for that matter. "Hello, Edward. Good to see you again."

"Hi."

"Is your lunch in your backpack?" Constance asked.

Again, he nodded.

"Okay then, off you go. You don't want to be late for the bus." Constance took his hand and walked him to the door. He reached up to give his nana a big hug, Constance squeezing him tight and kissing his forehead before letting him go. "Have a good day at school, sweetie."

Right before he strode out the door, he turned to Sophia and gave her a wide smile. "G-goodbye."

Touched by the boy's consideration, she tipped her head. "Bye, Edward."

Sophia finished her coffee and concluded her business with Constance, bidding her farewell and walking away from the kitchen's savory scents. In the well-designed lobby, her heels clicked on the stone floors as she headed toward her office. She still had difficulty believing that she owned any part of these elegantly rustic surroundings, yet each morning before she got out of bed, she reminded herself that half of the lodge belonged to her.

Luke appeared, seemingly out of nowhere, and walked alongside her. "Mornin'. Hey, can I speak with you a sec?"

"Good morning, Luke. I was going to call you this morning. How did your horse do last night?"

"She's gonna be okay. It was a tough delivery, but she managed. Her foal is real fine. You have to come see her."

"I will. You must be relieved."

"Surely am, but I think the mare might've struggled *less* than you did last night. I heard you had it rough after I left Kickin'."

"Oh," she said, her shoulders slumping. She wasn't thrilled she'd been the topic of discussion between the two brothers. Logan must have spilled all the beans with glee. "I see your brother told you I didn't handle the Number Three well."

Luke's face twisted with self-recrimination. "I should have never brought you there."

"Oh, no. It's not your fault. I should've known better. This has been a trying week for me, coming back here and dealing with all the changes in my life. Next time I'll do better."

"*Next* time? Honey, if you think I'm taking you back anytime soon—"

"I'm going back, Luke. One day."

His shoulders lifted in a dismissive shrug. "I'm just grateful that Logan was there to help you."

"Yes, your brother is my knight in shining armor," she grumbled quietly.

Luke threw his head back and laughed. Then she found humor in it, too, and laughed along with him. He took her arm and steered her out the front door. They strode along the length of the veranda and stood with the morning light to their backs as late spring sunshine warmed the air on a blue-sky day. Luke looked left then right, as if making sure they were alone. Whatever was on his mind today, he wanted a private conversation.

"I have an idea," he began. "Ruth's official last day of work is coming up. I'd like to throw her a surprise retirement party."

"That's nice of you, Luke. I'm sure she'd appreciate it."

"I'd like to do it at the house rather than the lodge. You know, get her out of the work environment. I was thinking out back, in our yard. Logan's thinking it's a good idea, too. The weather's been really nice at night."

"Go on." Sophia suspected that Luke was hinting that she be a part of his scheme, somehow.

"The thing is, Ruth usually coordinated our parties at the lodge, and well…I can't really ask her to do it. What I know about throwing a party can fit in my pinkie finger." He raised a work-roughened, rodeo-injured little finger.

So that was it. "You want my help?"

He fixed his gaze on her and shrugged. "I would *love* your help."

Sophia didn't have to think twice. "Of course."

Luke sighed with relief. "Great. You don't know how much I appreciate it. Funny, but I trust you more than the event planner we've used in the past. I want to make this special for Ruth."

"I'll do my best."

"It's not too much for you? You did just arrive. You have a new home and new job to settle into." Concern washed over his features as if he'd just realized what he was asking of her.

"I'm sure I can handle it. How many guests are we talking about here?"

"Probably sixty? We'd invite all the employees, although some will have to split shifts in order to stop by. There's several loyal patrons who have known Ruth from the beginning, and then there's her family. I'd like her grandkids to be invited, too."

"Okay. I could probably put that together. You want this to be a surprise?"

He glanced away for a second toward the pasture. "Yeah, I think so. Ruth wouldn't let us go to any fuss if she knew about it."

"I understand."

"Are you available tonight to go over the details? I'll bring dinner. No spice, no chili peppers, I promise."

Sophia was available every night. She had no hot dates, no friends other than Luke to hang out with, and putting together a party for Ruth would help her get to know the employees better, anyway. It was win-win. "Seven o'clock?"

"I'll be there."

Luke released a sigh of relief. "Thanks, Soph." He leaned forward to kiss her cheek chastely then smiled at her. "You're a lifesaver."

The knock came precisely at seven o'clock. Sophia's appetite had surged back to life this afternoon, and she was ready to share a delicious *bland* meal with a good friend. She had the table set for two and her laptop ready for the work they'd do on the retirement party. Sophia padded barefoot to the door, dressed comfortably in black capri pants and a white tank top tied at the side of her waist.

She opened the door with flair, eager for the company, and did an immediate double take, shaking her head and blinking.

"You're eyes aren't deceiving you." The comment spilled from Logan's tight lips. "It's not your pal Luke."

Sophia stared at the man standing on her doorstep. Her heart did a little flip. Her initial reaction to him still baffled her. Why was she so susceptible to him? He wasn't anything special, she reasoned. But then again, Sophia couldn't lie to herself. He was special in the ways that mattered to most women—smart, handsome, capable, kind to almost everyone else on the planet but her. And he was standing on her threshold with enough confidence to fill an arena. "What are you doing here?"

It wasn't the most mannerly greeting in the world. Even though her body reacted to Logan, she wasn't ready for another round of sparring. She'd looked forward to being with her friend this evening.

"There's been an accident. Luke's in the hospital."

Shocked, she gasped noisily as her hand flew to her chest. "Oh, my God. What happened?"

"A feisty stallion got loose this afternoon at the barn and Luke lost his footing trying to contain him. He was knocked down, and Trib nailed him good with both front hooves."

"Oh, no! How is he?"

"He's got three broken ribs, one broken arm and a concussion."

"I'm so sorry. Oh, poor Luke." Sophia's heart ached hearing the news about her friend.

"Luke's pretty tough, but all those rodeo injuries are surfacing again. He got hit pretty hard."

"Where is he?"

"Carson City Memorial."

"Can I see him?"

He shook his head. "The doctors sent me home. I've been with him all afternoon. He can't have any visitors tonight. They want him to rest. Someone will be observing him during the night for the concussion. With luck, they'll send him home tomorrow or the next day. He's going to be laid up for a while though."

Sophia realized she'd kept Logan out on the front porch. "Come in." She turned around and took a few steps into the parlor. "I'm so surprised." She'd wished Logan had called her from the hospital. She would've dropped everything to see Luke, but wishing for Logan to do anything for her was futile.

Logan followed her inside, his boot heels scraping against the floor. "Trib's a hard case and may be just as hardheaded as Luke. He's called Tribute in front of prospective buyers, but when they're out of hearing range we call him Tribulation. He's a grief maker. Of course, Luke's not blaming the dang horse. He blames himself for getting in the way."

Sophia turned to Logan, noticing for the first time that he held a white take-out bag.

"I feel terrible," she said.

"Your stomach aching again?"

"No, my stomach's fine. I feel bad for Luke. He doesn't deserve this."

"It was a freakish thing. Luke never lets a horse get the best of him. Nothing like this has happened before on the ranch."

"But he's going to be all right?" The thought of Luke in pain saddened her but she held back tears and told herself that Luke was strong and would probably heal quickly. At least, that was her rationalization. It was a small wonder that Logan hadn't blamed her for bringing Luke bad luck. And a small part of her wondered if that weren't truly the case. Luke befriends her and he winds up in the hospital. It was crazy to even consider it, yet Sophia couldn't deny the flash of guilt forcing its way into her thoughts.

"Yeah, eventually. He should make a full recovery."

"That's good news," she blurted. She couldn't hide her feelings. She cared about Luke.

Logan glanced at her with narrowed eyes, his mouth twitching, but whatever he was about to say to her he let drop. He strode past her and entered the kitchen. She followed him and watched as he removed items from the bag, placing them on the counter. "What's that?"

"Our dinner."

Any fool could see *and* smell the food he was arranging in the kitchen, but she never expected Logan to make the delivery and offer to eat with her. "Excuse me?"

"Don't be surprised. Was I supposed to argue with my brother about this?" He turned to her with recrimination in his eyes. "He made me promise to bring you dinner and work with you on Ruth's retirement party."

The air bottled up inside her lungs drained out. She was speechless.

"In fact, you and I are gonna have to pick up the slack at the lodge. Luke will be out of commission for a good long time."

Sophia walked to the counter, looking at the two dishes of pasta primavera Logan had taken out of the bag. Crusty Italian bread and a salad were also sitting on the counter.

"Meaning, we're going to have to work together from now on?"

Logan nodded, not looking happy about the prospect.

"He made you promise to be civil to me?"

Logan shrugged a shoulder. "Like I said, I'm not arguing with my brother when he's laid up."

"If you don't pull any more Ruth Polanskis on me, we might just manage working together."

Logan held back a devilish grin, but she saw the triumph in his eyes.

"Do we have a deal? For Luke's sake?" she asked, her hand
on one tilted hip. She did not approve of Logan's smug look,
no matter how hard he tried to conceal it.

Once again, Logan narrowed his eyes and gave her body
a long leisurely sweeping appraisal. When he did that, Sophia felt as if he were devouring her whole. It took him a
few seconds, but he finally agreed with a sharp nod. "For
Luke's sake."

Sophia stared at him for a moment and sighed silently.
They needed to eat quickly and get to work but she couldn't
resist asking, "Did he also tell you what food to bring?"

Logan's mouth twitched again. This time she might have
actually insulted him, but he took it in stride.

"No, I thought it up all by myself."

Okay, she thought, *I'll play nice.* She was hungry and
ready for food that wouldn't knock her socks off. "Looks
delicious."

Logan gave her the once-over again, his gaze fastening on
the three inch-strip of exposed skin at her waist. "Yep, can't
argue with that."

Sophia bit her tongue, holding back from giving him a
piece of her mind. She had a better way of getting even with
him. She wasn't forgetting about his ploy regarding Ruth Polanski. His scorching-hot gaze aside, she would have to show
him that she wasn't easy prey.

They sat eating quietly in her small alcove off the kitchen.
The linens were soft and white, the flowers wild from the
pasture, the glasses sparkling under the fading light. Sophia
was well aware of the handsome, uncompromising man sitting across the table from her. He'd brought a lovely meal
seasoned mildly so that it went down easily and soothed her
tender tummy. He'd also brought his underlying anger with
him. It was a given, but Sophia wouldn't let that stop her from
gobbling up everything on her plate. She'd played it safe and

hadn't put food in her stomach for nearly twenty-four hours and now she was looking for seconds.

Logan rose from the table and brought over the container of food. She scooped a few more spoonfuls onto her own plate, watching him as he held it. This was strangely nice.

Maybe Logan had the need to control every situation. Coming here to tell her about the accident had been done on his terms, not hers. He could have called her to explain about Luke. He could have alerted her that he would be coming by for dinner. Instead he chose to show up at her door unannounced.

As if reading her mind, he set down his fork and commented, "I never thought I'd be sitting in this kitchen, having dinner with you."

"Boggles the mind. Our second meal together in two nights." Sophia gave him a sweet smile, refusing to be intimidated.

"Let's not make a habit of this." He surveyed the rooms in his line of vision—the kitchen, parlor and hallway that led to the bedrooms. "I don't care for this place."

"The place is wonderful. It's me you don't care for. So just be honest about it."

Logan sipped water from his glass, and then eyed her carefully. "My brother kissed you today."

Sophia's radar went up. She'd promised herself she would be on guard around Logan, but now he'd dropped another bomb on her that she hadn't expected. "Did he tell you that?"

Logan glanced at her lips, and then lifted his lids to look her squarely in the eyes. "I was at the lodge this morning."

"So you saw Luke give me an innocent kiss and what?"

"Maybe I don't think anything about you is innocent."

Sophia's stomach began to ache, not from the food but from the conversation. Darn him for creating more turmoil in her belly. Logan liked playing judge and jury. In his mind, he'd already convicted her of a half-dozen crimes. "And why is that?"

"The apple doesn't fall far from the tree."

"So now I'm a cliché to you, Logan? I've already told you if you're comparing me to my mother, it's a compliment. She was a wonderful woman. I only wish I could be more like her."

"Yeah, well, I used to want to be like my father. Blind worship doesn't work. Sooner or later, you find out that the person you thought you knew wasn't that person at all."

It was pointless to argue with him. Sophia didn't want to spend her time defending herself or her mother. Logan's mind was made up and nothing she could say would change that. Even though she knew the truth about her mother and his father, he would never believe her. He didn't trust her, and she was through trying to gain that trust from him. Through trying to prove herself to him. The only thing she cared about was doing a good job at the lodge and proving to *herself* that she was worthy of Randall Slade's generosity.

"I'm sorry, Logan. It must have been a big blow for you to learn your father wasn't perfect. Most of us aren't, you know."

She rose from her seat and came over to his side of the table, brushing his shoulder to reach for his plate. Her long tresses flowed onto his lap as she brought her face inches from his. He smelled of earth, rawhide and musk, and her breathing quickened as their eyes met. He was a beautiful man who hated her, but right now, she saw desire darken his eyes and that did amazing, warm things to her sensitive belly. She was close enough that if she stumbled, she'd be lap dancing with Logan. The image didn't amuse her as much as it made her lust. She whispered gently, blowing her breath over his lips, playing the vixen he thought she was, "I'll clean this up, and then we'll get right to work so you won't have to stay any longer than necessary."

He stared at her, their gazes locked and then his hand

touched the ribbon of exposed skin at her waist. Her breath caught in her throat and her senses heightened as he splayed his fingers along the hem of her shirt. It was unexpected magic. Sophia relished the feel of him touching her. She didn't flinch or budge a muscle when Logan moved his hand in a soft caress that traveled back and forth over her midriff. She closed her eyes, mental goose bumps erupting in her mind. There was a connection between them, something raw and elemental and basic that defied logic or scrutiny. When he touched her, she reacted.

He made the tug that landed her on his lap and now the lap dance didn't seem so far off, didn't seem so outlandish in her mind. She felt the strength of his legs beneath her, the power of the hand that held her in place, while the other hand continued to make her body tingle.

She knew she shouldn't allow him this touch. She shouldn't allow him to get the upper hand again, but she was powerless to stop him. She craved the warmth and the thrill of Logan's caress. He managed to loosen the knotted fabric at her waist and she waited, filled with unabashed desire. He took a big swallow, his throat working while his hand slid underneath her top. Inch by inch, he moved his palm up her torso. Her nipples puckered in anticipation. The pulse between her legs throbbed. It was exquisite and sensual. She hadn't been with a man in years, not like this. The idea of Logan taking liberties with her body shocked her mind, but her body gave him all he wanted.

She arched her back, and wiggled slightly on his lap. His fingers pushed her bra down and her ample breasts spilled out. They were full, sensitized, and she waited for his touch. When it finally came she jerked slightly from the beautiful sensation. He palmed one breast, then the other, and a groan escaped from the depths of his throat. She murmured with pleasure, and squeezed her legs tight when his thumb rubbed over her nipple.

The pleasure was ripe and fresh and so greatly welcomed, but Sophia had to put a stop to this. She wouldn't give in to Logan. She couldn't give in to what they both craved. He would only turn it against her and make her life at Sunset Ranch unbearable. She didn't trust him. And she owed him for hurting her all those years ago.

Her breaths coming as heavy as his, she brought her hands to his face and leaned in close. This had to be her idea. When he tried to meet her lips, she pulled back a little, making sure he knew kissing him was her idea. This had to be her choice, her decision and on her terms.

She waited, and he backed off, then she brought her lips to his to sip first, and then draw out the moment. It was just as good as she'd remembered as an innocent girl of fifteen. Memories rushed forth of the glory and newness of Logan's kiss. His mouth accommodated hers now, just as before, but this time she was initiating the kiss. She pressed her mouth fully over his lips and deepened the connection. The world went a little fuzzy then. Logan's breath rushed out and he removed his hand from her breast. The loss was keenly felt. He wrapped his arm around her waist, and brought her up tight against his chest. Sophia took control again. She parted her lips, and slipped her tongue inside his mouth. She tasted him with a sweeping exploration and he joined in, their tongues mating.

Satisfied that Logan had relinquished control, Sophia couldn't let things go too far. Up until today, Logan had called all the shots. But putting a stop to Logan Slade's passion wasn't as easy as she thought it would be. He was a man who thrilled her and made her dizzy with desire. He, and only he, brought out an incredible, nearly insatiable hunger in her. Ever since the day that he'd first kissed her behind the gym, Sophia had dreamed of him and hated him at the same time for turning a beautiful memory into something sordid and obscene.

Summoning her willpower and abandoning the innate pleasure, she inched back, slowly pulling away from him until their lips were no longer locked.

Logan felt the loss, his gaze darting to her lips immediately. His expression changed from desire to determination. He reached for her, pulling her into a tight embrace. Crushing her to his chest, he slid his chair back; the jarring noise echoed against the stone floor. He stood, bringing her up with him. They faced each other now. A blaze of hunger lit his eyes, telling her he would take her here, right now.

A shocking thrill coursed through her body. Suddenly the battle lines got blurry, and she wondered if she was making a mistake in backing away. Everything fluid and tingling in her body said Yes to this man. Yet her mind told her to resist and not give Logan what he wanted. What *she* wanted. It would never be right between them.

"No, Logan," she whispered, nearly breathless. She put her hands firmly against him and pushed. The solid wall of his chest didn't budge. Frustrated, she took a step back, needing to create space between them. "We're not doing this. We can't."

He blinked and looked at her, the fire in his eyes replaced by an intense stare.

This had been a bad idea from the start. She was a ravaged mess with her shirt askew, her hair mussed and her lips bruised from his kiss. She realized too late that she'd played with fire. And she would get burned, too. Yet she couldn't relent. She had to stand her ground. It was the only way.

"Let me guess," he said with a rasp. "This is about getting even with me for high school and Ruth Polanski?"

Sophia closed her eyes. Her little payback plan had backfired. She refused to give him an answer. Instead, when her eyes opened, it was to look at his beautiful mouth wishing for things that would never be. Tension crackled in the air.

"Two brothers in one day, Sophia. Is that your style now?"

"Luke kissed me as a friend," she shot back quickly. "To

thank me for helping with Ruth's party." Why did it always come back to Luke? "It was a peck on the cheek and nothing more."

Logan frowned and his eyes filled with disgust. "And you kissed me, why? To prove a point? To get back at me for something stupid I did as a kid in high school?"

It was the first time she'd heard Logan refer to that time with regret. She nodded. "Yes, yes. I admit it, Logan. You needed a dose of your own medicine. You needed to come down off your throne and not pass judgment on me unfairly. I wanted to prove a point. You don't like it when the roles are reversed, do you? When you're the one being played?"

He heaved a breath, as if trying to temper his impatience. "Sweetheart, if you think I was being played," he said, pointing at her disheveled appearance, "then take a good look in the mirror. You enjoyed every second of my hands on you."

Shaking, Sophia fumbled to tie up her T-shirt and thread her fingers through her mussed hair. As she straightened herself out, she was aware of Logan's eyes on her. His statement was true—she'd nearly been ravaged by him before she'd come to her senses. Slowly, she lifted her lashes to look at him. "I…know."

He flinched. Her honesty surprised him and she witnessed a debate going on in the depths of his dark eyes. It was as if he were being pulled in two directions—either to take her back into his arms and finish what they'd started or to take his leave.

Moments ticked by.

Sophia watched him carefully, her body immobile. What she'd just admitted to him was ludicrous and yet it was the truth.

"Hell, I need some air," he said finally. He grabbed his hat, plunked it on his head and took a few steps toward the door. Then he pivoted to face her one last time. "We have to work together, Sophia. Meet me in my office tomorrow afternoon. We'll go over the plans then."

She gave him a brisk nod.

And then he was gone.

Five

With morning sunlight at his back, Logan gunned his truck, heading for Carson Memorial Hospital. He turned up the volume on the radio, trying to focus on the words of a Tim Mc-Graw song. But the lyrics didn't sink in. Instead, an image of Sophia Montrose sprawled across his lap, arching toward him, giving him access to her body, flashed into his mind. He couldn't drown those memories out with loud music. He couldn't concentrate on business ventures. No matter how much he'd tried, the recollection of Sophia's velvet-soft mouth brushing his, her firm flesh under his fingertips, the swell of her full, beautiful breasts in his palms continued to plague his thoughts.

Last night after leaving the cottage, he'd drowned out those images with a bottle of Jack Daniels. But today he'd hoped to hell he could fight the mental battles on his own. He refused to fall victim to Sophia Montrose, beautiful and desirable as she was, because he knew better. He'd seen what his father's love for a Montrose had done to his family.

When he'd been in high school he wanted to teach Sophia a lesson. He'd wanted to put her in her place. He'd wanted to lash out at her. He'd kissed her, never expecting that he'd be the one to learn a lesson. That kiss had startled him, and he'd been surprised at his own reaction to her. He'd never expected it to be so good. Sophia had made him feel as if he could conquer the world. And damn it, last night, and as much as he'd fought it, that same feeling had returned.

He reached the hospital, and pulled into a parking space, hoping a visit with Luke would clear his mind. He was concerned for his brother. Luke would heal from his injuries, but he'd be a bear to live with during his recovery.

Logan got out of his truck and strode purposefully through the front doors. He walked through the lobby, and took the elevator up. The doors opened to the third floor and, as he marched past a row of rooms, he kept his eyes trained straight ahead. He didn't like looking in on people in their sickbeds. His brother was too young to be laid up in a hospital. Though Luke had taken his share of tumbles while in the rodeo, he'd usually wound up getting patched up in the emergency room and sent on his way.

Logan reached his brother's room and stopped by the door to steal a look inside.

Luke had a smile on his weary face, a brighter expression than yesterday. It was a relief to see him looking a little better until Logan noticed that he wasn't alone. There was a reason for his brother's good mood.

Sophia was in the room.

She smiled at Luke, her gaze focused only on him as she moved toward his bed with a ribbon-tied bouquet of flowers in her hand. She stopped by the window next to his bed, standing at his shoulder, and gently moved a stray lock of hair from his forehead. Her soft melodic laughter wafted through the room.

Logan winced at the scene they made together. An image

of holding Sophia in his arms returned, and in that instant emotions he wouldn't name streamed into his consciousness.

He cursed aloud and both heads turned his way.

"Logan," his brother said in a weak voice. He managed a quick smile. "Come in."

As he walked into the room, Sophia made herself busy putting the flowers in a plastic water pitcher.

"How you doing?" he asked his brother.

"Pretty good today. Considering."

"You feel dizzy?" Logan asked. "The doc said you might for a few days."

"Not too much anymore. Wait, are there two of you standing there?"

"You're not funny," Logan said, though he was relieved to see Luke hadn't lost his sense of humor. He hated seeing his strong, good-natured brother reduced to wearing a tie-at-the-back hospital gown, lying on a remote-controlled sickbed. His right arm was in a cast, and three broken ribs didn't allow him to move much.

"Sophia says I am."

Logan shot Sophia a quick glance. She made eye contact with him for one second before focusing back on the flowers she was arranging. "Well, then it's gospel. You are."

"My brother is in full agreement with me? Doesn't happen every day."

"You're not laid up every day."

"Don't remind me. Once the meds wear off, I won't be smiling much."

"I hear you." Logan took a swallow. "You need anything?"

Luke shot him a pointed look. "Can you get me out of here today?"

"I take it your doc already told you no."

"Flat-out no. Thought you could pull some strings."

Logan put his hands out, palms up. "I didn't bring a rope."

"Now you're not funny." Luke closed his eyes then. Clearly,

the conversation was a strain on him, which only proved that Luke wasn't ready to come home. Knowing Luke, he wouldn't get much rest at the ranch. As much as he hated to admit it, Luke was better off in the hospital right now.

Sophia gave Luke a sympathetic look, her amber eyes forlorn. God, she was gorgeous, and so wrong for any of the Slade men that Logan felt the truth of it deep down in his bones. She was forbidden fruit, sure to poison any man who dared to take a bite. He wasn't entirely convinced she'd come to the hospital out of friendship and concern for his brother. He didn't trust her motives and it wasn't *just* because of his father's indiscretion with her mother. Sophia herself had married a rich old codger for his money. That fact couldn't be disputed.

Carefully, she put her hand on Luke's arm and he opened his eyes to look at her. "I'd better go now," she said. "I don't want to tax your strength."

He nodded. "I'm glad you stopped by. Thanks for the flowers."

She smiled warmly and bent to kiss his cheek. "I'll check on you later."

She picked up her purse, and gave Logan a cursory glance as she walked out of the room.

With his eyes closed again, Luke murmured, "What's up with the two of you anyway?"

Logan pulled a chair over to the bed and took a seat. He didn't pretend not to know what his brother was talking about. "Nothing's up. Why?"

"I'm injured, not blind." He snapped his eyes open. "You two looked...*guilty* about something."

"I hardly noticed her."

Luke's eyes drifted closed again. "Exactly. Sophia is hard *not* to notice. Did you have another fight?"

Just the opposite, he thought. They had...lust. And it'd been eating at Logan since their encounter last night. If Sophia had wanted retribution, she'd gotten her wish. "No. We didn't fight."

Luke took a long labored breath. His ribs must hurt like hell. Logan had broken a rib once as a kid, jumping out of a tree and hitting solid ground hard. He remembered breathing being really difficult for days.

"You working together okay?"

"Yeah, yeah," Logan said. "As a matter of fact, we're gonna work on Ruth's party later in the day."

"Just don't give her a hard time, okay?"

It was a good thing Luke's eyes were closed. He couldn't see Logan's mouth twist with annoyance. "Sure thing. We'll be right as rain. You just concentrate on getting some rest. I'll come by later on."

Luke turned his head to the side and slowly nodded. "I'm coming home tomorrow, doctor or no doctor."

Logan knew he meant business. Nothing much kept his brother down.

Sophia spent the morning going over upcoming events at the lodge with Ruth. There was the annual Memorial Day barbecue, marking the beginning of the summer season, as well as a wedding planned in the first week of June. Sophia took notes, reviewed the ledgers and read the week's guest surveys to see if there was anything they could improve on. She made her daily rounds inside the lodge, checking on the staff, and then strolled outside to meet with sunshine and warm fresh air.

So far, so good, she thought as she stood on the veranda, looking out at the newly blossoming garden, the green pastures and beyond. Everywhere her eyes touched belonged to the Slades but for the dazzling Sierra Nevadas. Now she was a small part of that empire. Being half owner of the lodge brought her a fuller range of responsibilities than managerial duties and although it was a bit daunting, Sophia had geared herself up for the challenge.

She strode past the gates and headed for the stables. One of the services of the lodge was to offer guided horse rides on the property, and Sophia held a revised schedule on her clipboard.

Just as she arrived, Hunter Halliday rounded the barn wall, and stopped three inches short of bowling her over. Stunned, she leaned way back, the clipboard flying out of her hands as she lost her balance. Hunter reached for her, his hands firm and steady on her shoulders to right her.

"Oh, Ms. Sophia. Didn't see you coming."

He was taller than her by five inches and broad-shouldered for a boy of seventeen. She had to look up at him. "It's all right. I didn't see you, either."

"As long as you're okay," he said, giving her body a quick scan. Once he realized his hands were still on her, he removed them quickly, and blushed red under his tanned skin.

She straightened herself out, took a breath and thought to ease Hunter's mind by getting right down to business. "I'm fine, really. I need to run something by your dad." She bent to retrieve the clipboard off the ground. When she came up holding it, Hunter appeared perplexed that he hadn't thought to pick it up himself.

He blinked. "Sorry."

"No problem. Is your dad here by any chance?"

"Nope," he said. "Dad's at the ranch today."

"Actually, maybe you can help me. Will you check over this new schedule, and tell me if it looks okay? I made some changes." She handed him the clipboard.

Hunter seemed relieved that she'd moved on to business. "Sure, I can do that."

"No hurry. If you want to bring it by the office tomorrow morning, that's soon enough."

"I'll do that."

"Thank you. Oh, and Hunter…good catch. I might have fallen on my butt if you hadn't caught me."

Hunter smiled shyly. "I wouldn't have let that happen."

Sophia walked away from the barn thinking that Ward Halliday had raised a well-mannered boy.

Her mood brightened even more when she spotted Edward across the yard with Blackie at his heels. The boy tossed a ball and Blackie took off running.

Sophia came up just as Blackie returned. "Hello, Edward."

"Hi," he said.

"No school today?"

He shook his head. "It's p-parent's day."

Sophia immediately ached for Edward. Neither one of his parents would show up for the parents' conference today. His teacher wouldn't share with them his strengths and weaknesses in the classroom. They wouldn't hear about his behavior and his homework habits. They wouldn't come home feeling proud of his accomplishments. Sophia hid her sorrow for the boy. She reminded herself that he had Constance. His grandmother was determined to make sure Edward knew he was loved. "That means it's really kids' day."

The boy grinned, and Blackie jumped up against Edward's lanky frame, pleading for another ball toss. Edward didn't disappoint. He threw the ball and the dog went running again. "I g-get to play with B-Blackie and then go o-on a h-hike with Mr. Slade."

Sophia winced inwardly. Logan was compassionate with the boy. She was glad of it, but seeing that side of Logan only confused her more. "Where do you hike?"

Edward pointed to a low rise on the mountains. "Up th-there."

"And does Blackie get to go?"

"Yep."

"Sounds like fun."

Edward gave her a thoughtful look. "W-want to come?"

Sophia was touched by the invitation. "Oh, uh…"

"Ms. Montrose has work to do."

Sophia whirled around, startled by the sound of Logan's voice. It was the second time today she'd been nearly bowled over. "Logan, where did you come from?"

He grinned. "Same place as everybody else."

She wanted to slap the crooked smile off his face, until he looked at Edward with warmth in his eyes, and ruffled the boy's hair.

"Hi there. You enjoying your day off from school?" Logan asked.

"Yes, sir." The dog jaunted back and Edward pulled the ball from his mouth.

"Good. You get your chores done, and I'll come get you in three hours. We'll go on that hike, okay?"

"Okay," he said.

Edward tossed the ball toward the barn, and then ran as fast as he could to catch up to the dog that had dashed after it. Once he'd gotten a good thirty feet away, he turned and waved to Sophia.

Sophia waved back, and watched him until he entered the barn.

"You're good with the boy," Sophia said, not realizing she'd spoken the words aloud.

Logan clucked his tongue. "As opposed to being down-right mean and rotten?"

Sophia snapped her head up, annoyed at Logan for sucking the joy out of a purely innocent comment. "It's a wonder you can stand up straight with that giant chip on your shoulder."

He put his head down, stared at his boots and sighed heavily. "Yeah, I suppose you're right. You paid me a compliment and—"

"You found something sinister in an honest observation."

Logan's dark brows lifted, creasing his forehead. "You make me sound like a devil."

Since when did Logan care *what* she thought of him? She searched his eyes and with a shake of her head admitted, "I don't think you're mean."

He looked away, unwilling to share a poignant moment with her, unwilling to realize that she didn't hold harsh feelings for him the way he did for her. "Edward has had a rough childhood. His parents have made bad choices, and the boy shouldn't have to pay for that."

As he spoke, she noted the pain in Logan's voice. For a brief moment, she wondered if Logan related to Edward because he'd had pain in his life, too. Pain she was certain he attributed to her mother's relationship with his dad. "Life isn't always fair," Sophia said.

He stared at her. "No, it isn't."

Sophia balked at his negative tone. This conversation was going nowhere. "I'd better get back to work."

She brushed by him, but before she was out of his reach, he took hold of her arm, his fingertips gently digging into the flesh. His touch stirred her senses. She paused for a second, sensations rippling through her body. On a silent sigh, she turned to face him. "What?"

"I've got appointments all afternoon, and the hike with Edward later. We have to talk about Ruth's party sometime."

"Your schedule is busier than mine. Tell me when, and I'll be there."

"First thing tomorrow morning. Come to my office at 8:00 a.m. sharp."

Logan's home office was private, so there'd be no chance of Ruth catching on. She'd never suspect a thing and that was the whole point of the surprise. Sophia dreaded being alone with Logan, yet what choice did she have—they were partners. "I'll be there."

He released his gentle hold on her and she walked away. But the impact of Logan's touch stayed with her for the remainder of the workday.

Well past seven o'clock, she closed up her office and left the lodge as the sun made one last blazing hurrah on the horizon. She enjoyed the glorious sunset on the walk home. But when she climbed the steps leading up to her front door, just as she put her key into the lock, a rustling sound from behind her interrupted her peace. She felt a presence. Someone was in the bushes. She turned sharply to see who it was. "Is someone there?" she called out.

No one appeared. There was no response. In the fading light she scanned the area, searching the garden, shrubs and thicket of trees and then farther, past the yard. Had she imagined it? With her back turned, she'd been so certain that someone was approaching from behind. An eerie sensation crept up her spine.

For a moment, she stood perfectly still, listening. A lump formed in her throat and before she allowed butterflies to take flight in her stomach, she gave herself a mental talking to. *Don't let your imagination go wild. No one is out there. It was probably the wind.*

Though at the moment, not so much as a breeze blew by.

Sophia shook off the feeling of déjà vu, turned the doorknob and flipped on the light switch as she entered the house, making sure to lock the front door. She moved carefully through the rooms, looking around, and finally decided she was being silly. She was safe on Sunset Ranch. There were security gates, and the property was well guarded.

But just in case, Sophia slept with the lamp on that night.

The next morning, Sophia stood at the cottage's entranceway, staring at a plain piece of folded, white computer paper she'd lifted from the welcome mat outside her door. Curious, she glanced out to the yard, looking to find someone who might have left her a note. Coming up empty in her search, she unfolded the paper quickly and read four words typed above the crease.

She blinked, and reread the note.

Her shoulders slumped, and her breath came in shortened bursts. "Oh…no."

Slight tremors coursed through her body, and she fought the sensations, trying to make sense of what she'd found. The words were not threatening—should not instill panic. And yet she couldn't tamp down her fear. She couldn't believe this was happening to her…again.

You are very beautiful.

Last night, she'd been certain someone had been watching her. And today, as she'd slipped into her brown slacks and sleeveless cream blouse after her morning shower, she'd realized how foolish she'd been.

"Don't be paranoid, Sophia," she'd said into the bathroom mirror, tying her long hair back into a loose braid. "You heard a frightened animal dash from the yard or a bird flitting through the branches of the tall pines." She had herself convinced it was nothing. But after seeing those four words, Sophia feared her world could very well tip upside down. She wasn't convinced or sure of anything anymore. There was only one conclusion she could come to.

Someone *had* been outside her cottage last night.

Someone was watching her.

Sophia squinted against the morning sunshine, looked around the yard once again and then shut the door. Her legs wobbly, she made her way to the sofa and lowered herself onto it.

She closed her eyes.

She had to get a grip.

Yet she couldn't move or summon up the energy to start her busy day. Her mind flashed to two years ago and that very frightening time in her life.

Shortly after her mother's cancer treatments had begun, she'd landed a position on the chorus line for the Las Vegas Fantasy Follies. Hospital bills had piled up faster than she could work them off. She'd been scared and worried about a mother who was in major denial about the severity of her illness. Out of necessity, Sophia had become both a worried, doting daughter and the only breadwinner for their little family.

When the first note had arrived to her dressing room, Sophia hadn't thought much of it. Her mind was on her mother's chemo treatments…and kicking her legs high enough and in sync with the other dancers in order to keep her job. Two more notes had followed. After she'd received the third note delivered to the dressing room, her closest friend in the follies remarked, "Oh, wow, Sophia. You have yourself a stalker."

It was then that Sophia had learned that propositions usually came to showgirls in face-to-face encounters with gentlemen backstage after the show. They weren't typed out on unadorned, *untraceable* white computer paper.

The notes kept coming sporadically; there was no rhyme or reason to them. Sophia had gotten spooked on several occasions when she was sure there was one particular pair of eyes in her audience with deeper, more observant, more sinister motives than watching pretty girls dance, jiggle and tease on a glitzy stage. There were other times when she felt as if she were being followed home, although she'd never seen a soul. Her life had been one great big ball of fear. Fear for her mother, fear for her job, fear for her safety. She'd called the police once, and they'd taken a report noting her complaint, but they said no crime had been committed and Sophia figured she was pretty much on her own.

Until Gordon Gregory had come to her rescue, her greyhaired knight in shining armor.

Gordon felt he owed the Montrose women a great debt for saving his granddaughter's life. Months prior, Louisa had taken in a wayward girl who had run away from her parents' home in Northern California. She'd shown up in the alley behind the motel Louisa managed, high on drugs and

beaten pretty severely from a mugging. The girl had been a
runaway for certain and might have died on the backstreets
of Las Vegas if Louisa and Sophia hadn't taken her in and
nursed her back to health. The frightened girl threatened to
run again if they called the police. They hadn't. Instead they'd
talked to her for three days straight and gained her trust, making her see that she had hit rock bottom. But she still had a
chance to save herself, and once she agreed to go home and
make a fresh start, they'd learned that the misguided teenager
was Amanda Gregory, granddaughter to Gordon Gregory, a
wealthy oil magnate who had a home in Las Vegas.

Gordon was so grateful to Louisa and Sophia for saving
Amanda that he'd offered to give them anything they wanted.
The sky was the limit.

"We shouldn't be rewarded for doing the right thing," her
ailing mother had told him.

After that, Gordon had become a friend. And when things
got bad and the two Montrose women had really needed help,
Gordon had intervened with his offer to take Sophia away
from the Follies and any danger she might have been in,
marry her and give Louisa the best possible health care. The
older gentleman had principles and old-fashioned notions
about marriage, despite his four failed unions and the big age
difference. He'd insisted there would be no strings attached
initially if Sophia was in agreement. He'd offered her time
to adjust to the marriage and a safe haven from all her worries. At the time, with skyrocketing medical bills, a would-
be stalker and an ill mother on her hands, Sophia had had no
choice. Basically, Gordon had been the answer to her prayers.
Sophia had even managed to convince her mother that she'd
be happy with Gordon, but in truth, she'd wanted to give her
mother peace of mind that her daughter would be well cared
for if anything happened to her.

The marriage was to be a quiet affair. But the details of

her marriage had been leaked to the tabloids, which naturally resulted in splashy front-page headlines. Sophia was not painted in a good light—the twentysomething gold-digging showgirl married to the aging oil magnate. At the time, Sophia had been out of options and her mother's health had been foremost in her mind.

Sophia wasn't always proud of her decisions. There were times when deep remorse set in. Her choices may not have always been wise, but she'd done what she'd had to do, out of necessity.

She would not go back to living in fear.

Slowly, methodically Sophia squeezed the note in her palm, her fingers digging in until the paper curled into an abstract form. She watched the words crumple away as she tightened her fist and then gave a final squeeze. The wrinkled lump in her hand couldn't hurt her anymore. It couldn't cause her any anguish now.

She would have to forget about this and hope it was a fluke. A mere coincidence. After all, it had been the other sentence absent from this note that had changed a compliment into a threat. Today's note didn't say "You will be mine one day."

Sophia clung to that notion.

Still shaken, she rose from the sofa and moved to the kitchen, where she pressed her toe to the foot pedal of the stainless-steel garbage can. The note belonged in the past. She wouldn't allow it to terrify her. She wouldn't give it credence. Not here, not now. She was trying to rebuild her life on Sunset Ranch. With one forceful toss, the note was history. The lid of the garbage can slammed shut, and Sophia put the ordeal out of her mind. She grabbed her purse, slung it over her shoulder and walked out of the cottage on legs that moved solely by steely, stubborn conviction.

She would not allow that note to destroy her day.

Ten minutes later she couldn't say the same thing about Logan Slade.

* * *

"You're late, Sophia. What part of eight sharp don't you understand?"

Sophia winced at Logan's demeaning tone. He was lecturing her as if she were a student in his classroom, sounding uncannily like Mr. Anderson in ninth-grade history.

Tardiness will only get you detention for the day. You make me wait, and I make you wait.

"You're right," she said, taking a seat to face him from across his office desk. "I'm sorry. It won't happen again." Sophia set her shoulder bag down on the seat next to her and opened up her valise, drawing out a clipboard.

Logan's angry tone ebbed. "You look pale. Didn't you sleep last night?"

Sophia straightened in her seat. The darn note had rattled her more than she'd have thought. On the short drive to Logan's house, she'd been reliving the past—thinking of her mother, her life and her bad choices. Her nerves were almost shot and she had to put on a good front for Logan not to see her distress. For all her bravado, Sophia felt things stronger than she let on and it manifested in a trembling body and a distracted mind. "I slept wonderfully, thank you."

"*Sorry* and *thank you,* all in the thirty seconds since you've been here, Sophia?"

Her chin went up. "Would you rather that I tell you how rude you were to me when I walked in?"

Logan grinned as if he'd coaxed the response he'd wanted from her. "I expect promptness."

"In a perfect world, maybe you should."

"What's not so perfect about your world?"

Sophia gazed down at the floor. She wouldn't answer Logan's question, but she was tempted to. She would love to tell him the truth about her imperfect life, and make him see that she was not the sordid, calculating woman he thought her to be. Not that he'd believe her. His mind was made up. "We don't have enough time in the day."

"Good point," he said, studying her for a moment before glancing at his watch. "Let's get down to business. I have another meeting in an hour."

Glad the focus was off her, Sophia discussed her ideas about the surprise party, how she thought they could pull it off without Ruth knowing and her plans for the menu and decorations. Uncharacteristically, Logan agreed with her about everything. She was pleased that he chose not to argue the details. When it came to throwing a party, Logan didn't have a clue. He was smart enough to defer to her. Yet she had a hard time focusing one hundred percent of her attention on the task at hand when her thoughts today were on the past.

She missed her mother. She still couldn't believe she was gone. Oftentimes, she'd wanted to pick up the phone to call her.

Hey, Mama, I finally got your chili recipe right.

Hey, Mama, the daisies are in full bloom outside your bedroom window.

Hey, Mama, I just wanted to say good morning.

The loss was so keen that it always took Sophia a few seconds to realize that she would never be able to call her mother again.

"Sophia?" Logan's voice broke through her thoughts.

She snapped her head up. "Oh, uh… Yes?"

His brows gathered as he aimed a pointed question at her. "Something's up with you today. What's going on?"

Sophia stared into Logan's deep, dark eyes. For half a second, she wanted to confide in him about the mysterious note and how it had stirred bad memories for her. "I, uh—"

His gaze drifted down to her hand holding the pen. She'd forgotten to bring her laptop, something Logan had probably noticed but hadn't mentioned. She took notes the old-fashioned way today, and her hand trembled as she jotted things down.

"Nothing. I missed breakfast. I guess I'm a little shaky." That was the truth. She hadn't eaten this morning and it was a good enough reason to give him.

Although he gave her a nod of understanding, the entire time they spoke, she felt Logan's gaze penetrating her, watching and waiting for a hint to indicate why she was acting so out of character. He was, by nature, suspicious of her. And no amount of explanation would convince him to be otherwise.

Once the plans were set for the party, they moved the discussion to her progress with the lodge. Sophia forced herself to concentrate on details for the next fifteen minutes, and they concluded their business within the hour.

Logan rose from his desk, hawklike eyes watching her every move. She rose, too. Thankfully, her legs were stronger now, and her nerves not quite so raw. She had a full day of work ahead of her and a party to plan.

"I'll call you tonight to check on the progress," he said.

Sophia slipped her purse strap over her shoulder. "Fine." He came around his desk to meet her, and walked her toward the door. "How is Luke this morning?" she asked.

"Better, from what the doctors tell me."

"Is he coming home today?" Sophia couldn't keep hope out of her voice, which garnered a tight-lipped response from Logan. "If he has anything to say about it, he will."

"Give him my best when you see him."

"Will do," he said as they reached the office door. "Oh, and Sophia."

"Hmm?"

"Eat something. Can't have Sunset Lodge's manager faint dead away in the middle of the lobby."

Sophia sent him a sugary-sweet smile. "Thanks for your concern."

"Anytime."

Sophia had the distinct feeling that Logan Slade had his eyes trained on her backside as she walked out of his office and down the hall.

"I'll go crazy if I stick around here much longer." Luke's frustrated words issued from his mouth in a whisper.

Poor guy, Sophia thought. He couldn't move too much in his bed without feeling tremendous pain. Yet he stubbornly refused to take the meds the doctor had prescribed for him.

"You have to give yourself some time, Luke," Sophia said. "You've been home only a few days."

"Can't do a damn thing on the ranch, either. With my cracked ribs and this here busted-up arm."

Sophia glanced at the cumbersome cast that went more than halfway up his right arm and couldn't argue the point. Luke wasn't one to sit still, yet what option did he have? He'd ridden the rodeo circuit and from what she'd gathered he'd never suffered an injury like this before. "What you need is something to take your mind off your troubles." Sophia leaned toward him to bring a freshly baked butter cookie dusted with powdered sugar near his mouth. "Here, try one of these," she said. "I made them early this morning for you."

Luke's gaze lowered to the cookie hovering by his lips. "Smells delicious. Lay it on me."

He opened his mouth, and she inserted the cookie. He took a bite and chewed thoughtfully, then swallowed and sighed with appreciation, laying his head back against the bed pillow. "You're an angel, Sophia."

Too bad his brother didn't think so. She was an angel to Luke, and the devil's spawn to Logan. One wouldn't think the two men had the same blood running through their veins.

"That cookie melted in my mouth. Gotta be the best cookie I've ever had." Then he added, "Don't be telling Constance I said so."

She put the rest of the cookie into his mouth. Her mother's

recipe never failed to make people smile. "I made two dozen,"
she said, gesturing with a head tilt toward the plate on his
nightstand, sitting next to the bouquet of flowers she'd brought
him when he first arrived from the hospital. "You can thank
me later, after you've finished all of them."

Luke's left hand came out to take hers. "I can thank you
now—"

"No problem, I love to bake—"

"For coming to see me twice already since I've been
home," he rasped out. "And for listening to me moan and
groan."

"That's what friends are for."

Morning sunshine streamed in through the shuttered windows facing east. But the beautiful day didn't have an effect
on Luke's sour mood. He was a man accustomed to being
on the move. "There'll be a hell of a lot more moaning and
groaning," he confessed.

"I know. I can't blame you. But you'll heal. You have to be
patient." Sophia moved from the chair to the side of his bed,
carefully lowering down so as not to disturb him. "Here,"
she said, leaning forward and offering him a second cookie.
"Have another."

He bit down, and closed his eyes while he chewed. "How
are things at the lodge?" he asked quietly.

A pipe had burst, leaking water into the rooms on the
second floor, the smoke alarm had gone off for no apparent
reason in the kitchen and one of the guests had slipped and
sprained an ankle while stepping down from their saddle
since Luke's accident. Business as usual, she mused. "It's
coming along."

"Glad to hear it. You fit right in on Sunset Ranch."

Sophia sighed. "I love it here."

"And I love that you're here, feeding me cookies."

She laughed and Luke cracked a smile, but a second later,

he paid for the movement with a grimace of pain. Sophia grimaced, too, sympathizing with him.

"Is there anything I can do for you before I go to work?" she asked.

Luke shook his head. "Nope. You go on. Thanks for the visit and the cookies."

"I spoiled your breakfast."

"You spoiled me, period."

"I'll come back again soon."

"I might not be here."

Sophia thought he was kidding until she saw a spark of determination in his eyes. "Where would you be?"

"An old rodeo buddy of mine is recovering from a bad injury. Broke his back a while ago. He's got a cabin on the north shore of Tahoe and is itching for a drinking partner. I'm thinking on it. I'm gonna be pretty darn useless around here for the next couple of weeks."

"Can you travel?"

"I can if I take those dang pills. It's not a far trip. Logan offered to drive me if I decide to go. He thinks it's a good idea. Wants me outta his hair, from all the complaining I've been doing."

Sophia shook her head. "I'm sure your brother wants what's best for you. Will you let me know if you decide to go? I'd want to say goodbye."

"Sure thing."

Sophia rose from the bed gingerly, and gave him one last look before exiting the room. She moved through the house with familiarity, as if it was only yesterday that she'd played in these stately paneled rooms and raced down the hallways on her way out the kitchen to a backyard that had doubled as an amusement park in her childhood.

The Slades had a tree house that looked like a Western fort with a steep slide and rubber swings. They had bicycles and wagons and a giant fenced-off pool. They owned horses and had been taught from an early age to respect animals, and all of their other possessions, as well. Sophia had often heard Mr. Slade instruct his boys, "Take care of things, or be prepared to lose them."

The boys took it strictly as a warning then, but later in life Sophia realized how smart Randall Slade had been. He'd meant it as a life lesson.

Sophia had almost reached the front door when Logan's deep voice stopped her cold. "Sophia, I'd like a word with you. Got a second?"

His words echoed in the entryway as Sophia slowly pivoted on her three-inch heels. She found Logan striding toward her, his face a mask of indifference but for a jaw that twitched as he approached.

Her heart skipped a beat at the sight of him. She asked herself, why him? Why did she find him so darn attractive when clearly the two of them would never happen? Logan had a perfectly gorgeous, fun-loving sibling whom Sophia adored, but Luke didn't make butterflies take flight in her belly or make her nerves jump and her body tingle the way Logan did.

He'd touched her intimately the other night.

And she'd wanted more.

Irritated at her train of thought, she gave him a terse response. "I'm on my way to the lodge."

"Busy?"

"I have some issues that need tending. Yes, I'm very busy."

His mouth curved up in a casual smile that belied his words. "But not too busy to hand-feed my brother your cookies."

Sophia blinked, surprised that Logan had known about that. "Were you spying on me?"

He took her question matter-of-factly. "I'd hardly call it spying. It's my house. I passed by Luke's room and saw the two of you in there. Cozy little picture you made."

Sophia closed her eyes briefly, praying for patience. Damn

him. She would not let Logan get the best of her. "Luke enjoyed my cookies. You should try one. They are delicious."

His eyes moved over her, gently caressing each curve of her body. The dress she wore today was clingy and cranberry-red and Logan could hardly miss the fact that Sophia had forgotten to wear her usual matching jacket that concealed her cleavage somewhat. She felt exposed to his gaze. He touched every inch of her with eyes that devoured, eyes that held a thrilling promise. "Maybe I want my own batch, Sophia."

The underlying sensuality of his comment fascinated her. She put her head down, her gaze catching the shiny polished tips of his black snakeskin boots. Rugged, rough-edged and appealing, Logan Slade made mincemeat of her resolve. She raised her head slightly, not quite able to meet his eyes. Instead she stared at the tanned skin exposed by the opened collar of his chambray shirt. She replied in a broken, quiet whisper. "Maybe…one day, Logan."

He put his hand under her chin. With the tips of his fingers, he lifted her face a fraction of an inch until she was forced to look into his eyes. They smoldered like dark coals and sent a warm shot of heat through her body. It wasn't fair that Logan could do her so much damage with a mere look, a single tender touch.

He bent his head and Sophia pleaded with him. "Don't… don't kiss me."

He inched closer. "You want me to."

She did. She wanted him to kiss her. She wanted him to make her feel the way he had the other night.

The lap dance night.

"Logan, you out there?" Luke's strained voice broke through their moment like a cold splash of water.

Logan cursed quietly.

Sophia swallowed down hard.

Both looked in the direction of Luke's bedroom.

"Yeah, I'm here," Logan called back to him. "I'm coming."

Six

Sophia never had the chance to say goodbye to Luke. He left the night after her visit to deliver the cookies. Logan had thought it best for Luke to travel late at night so that he could sleep during the trip to Tahoe. Apparently, from what she could gather, his host, Casey Thomas, was a good guy, wild in his younger rodeo days, but now a big fan of the simple life. The two would drink and shoot the breeze at Casey's lakeside cabin.

But as Sophia gazed out the window of her cottage this evening, dressed and ready for Ruth's surprise party, she felt Luke's absence in the pit of her stomach. He'd been gone for five days and she'd spoken to him twice in that time, but she hadn't confided in him. Since he'd left, she'd received two more notes on her doorstep.

You are very beautiful.

The notes were always folded neatly and always typed on plain white computer paper. While receiving one note might have been a fluke and something she could ignore, receiving two more meant that whoever was out there, whoever was sending these notes was persistent. She feared they would continue to torment her. She'd been sleeping with the lights on lately. She'd been listening intently for out-of-the-ordinary sounds in and around the cottage.

Sophia let go a deep breath to steady her nerves. Tonight, she would play an integral role in getting Ruth to her surprise party. Sophia had worked her buns off this week, making arrangements, hiding a drastic change in employees' schedules from Ruth and working with Logan and his staff to get the Slade home ready for the party.

The cover story was that Ruth and Sophia were to meet one of Randall Slade's high-profile friends who was interested in using Sunset Lodge as a summer retreat for the entire staff of a private college. Sophia had explained that Logan would first host a special dinner at the Slade ranch house to impress the client, then one of Ruth's last duties would be to help Sophia put him up for the night at the lodge and give him the royal treatment tomorrow.

Ruth bought the entire concept and Sophia was certain she didn't have a clue what was really going on. Sophia was on pins and needles, though. Without Luke here for support, being secretive with Ruth all week and receiving another one of those notes made her jumpy.

Before exiting the cottage, Sophia scanned the property thoroughly, just like she'd been doing all week long. She grabbed her wrap and her purse and looked around one last time before locking up the cottage and getting into her car. She had no proof or evidence to back her feeling of being watched, other than that one night when she heard a disturbance in her yard, yet Sophia felt the sensation deep down in her bones.

Thirty minutes later, after picking up Ruth, who was dressed very elegantly in a cobalt-blue and silver dress, Sophia delivered Ruth to the Slade home.

Logan answered the door personally, dressed in a dark Western suit and string tie—a handsome maverick with a charming smile. Upon spotting Ruth, he gave her a welcoming kiss on the cheek, and then gave Sophia a quick approving nod as his razor-sharp gaze raked over her upswept hair, shimmery sequined cocktail dress and sandaled feet.

"Our guest is outside. He is anxious to meet with you both." Logan stepped between them, offering the ladies his arm. With Ruth chatting amiably on his right and Sophia on his left, the three of them walked through the wide parlor double doors to be greeted by the sight of twinkling lights, grandly decorated tables and about sixty of Ruth's friends and coworkers.

"Surprise!" the gathered crowd shouted in unison, stunning Ruth into silence. Tears filled her eyes. With her hand to her chest, she truly appeared surprised.

Logan and Sophia looked at each other. For a brief moment in time they shared the triumph. They'd pulled it off.

The festivities got under way quickly. Ruth was swarmed by guests giving their congratulations, kisses and loving hugs. She was the center of attention, as she should be, with her husband, her children and grandchildren by her side.

Sophia took a minute for herself. She strolled to the edge of the beautifully landscaped yard. Beyond the whitewashed wooden fences illuminated by strings of tiny lights was pasture land that stretched for miles. It was so vast and remote, so steeped in eerily quiet darkness that a chill ran down her spine. She shivered in the warm night and rubbed her hands up and down her arms, attempting to bank her feelings of uncertainty. Those anonymous notes were weighing on her and affecting her daily routine. She couldn't get them off her mind.

"Need some quiet time?"

The voice from behind made her jump.

She whirled around. "Oh!"

Logan's face was cast in shadows, making him look sinister, but oddly enough his comment had been soft and calming. "Apparently not, since you're here now."

Logan flashed a smile. His expression wasn't one of battle. He offered her one of the two crystal champagne flutes he held in his hand. "Here, have a drink."

Sophia shook her head. "I don't…drink."

"It's sparkling cider."

Thoughtful, Sophia mused.

As he handed her a glass, his fingers caressed hers, and she felt the impact of his touch down to her toes. "Thank you."

"To Ruth," he said, and then added, "and to you. You pulled off a great surprise party."

Warmed by the compliment, she brought her glass to his with a gentle clink. "Thank you. But you helped."

"Very little."

He was being magnanimous tonight. Sophia welcomed it, but as she brought the drink to her mouth, her hand trembled. She still hadn't gotten over her initial bout of nerves. Or was it Logan making her nervous?

"What's wrong with you, Sophia? You've been jumpy for days."

Logan had noticed.

Sophia turned to face the bleakness of the distant pasture. She couldn't look at Logan now. She was weak and vulnerable at the moment, and tears welled in her eyes. It was ridiculous that a little kindness shown by Logan Slade could bring on so much sentiment. "It's nothing that concerns you."

He moved closer. His presence surrounded her from behind. "You admit there is something?" His warm breath caressed her earlobe.

Sophia squeezed her eyes closed.

"Answer me, Sophia," Logan said.

He made her believe he cared about her. Why else would he question her? But Sophia couldn't place much faith in Logan's motives. She'd learned that lesson long ago. If the notes persisted, then Sophia would confide in a Slade, but the man she would tell would be Luke.

Sophia spun around to face Logan. "We should get back to the par—"

"Miss S-Sophia, Mr. Logan." Edward came running toward them, his face animated. The night's breeze fluffed the wisps of his hair as he approached. "L-look what just came. It's a g-giant f-flower horse! Y-you have to s-see it!"

When he reached her, Sophia crouched down to his level. His eyes, lit with excitement, lightened Sophia's heavy mood. "Hi, Edward. So what is this we have to see?"

"A h-horse made of f-flowers. It's as b-big as a real h-horse. Mr. Luke sent it for the p-party. Y-you have to s-see it."

Sophia glanced at Logan. His lips twisted, but he didn't let on to Edward that he'd interrupted a private conversation.

"Would you like to show it to me?" Sophia asked.

Edward's head bobbed up and down.

Sophia chuckled and put out her hand. Edward looked into her eyes first, then shyly took her hand. "Lead the way, my friend."

Edward took off at a fast pace, with Sophia running on the tips of her toes to keep up.

She assumed Logan was somewhere behind them, making his way back to the festivities.

Secretly, Sophia was grateful for the interruption.

Or should she call it an escape?

Logan swirled bourbon and soda in a tumbler, his shoulder braced against the patio pillar, his gaze keenly fastened on Sophia. She swayed her hips in time with the music on the dance floor and caught the attention of every male at the party, married or not. Even the damn disc jockey was eyeing her. How could he blame them? She was a stunner in a black-sequined dress that shimmered under the festive party lights. At this time, in that dress, Sophia couldn't conceal her luscious form. She didn't try to cover herself up with a jacket or sweater. She was a curvy glamour queen with her hair up in a tangle, held together by rhinestone clips.

Gorgeous.

Hunter had her in his arms now. Every so often, she would smile at him, making mush of the poor kid. She'd already danced with Ward, Ruth's husband and young Edward. She appeared to be having a great time, but there was something underlying, something not quite right about her tonight.

When she wasn't in the limelight, her expression held tension. He'd seen her dart cautious glances around, as if watching for something or someone.

Lately, every time he'd approached her she'd just about jumped out of her skin. It wasn't his concern, unless what was troubling her had something to do with Sunset Ranch.

Then it mattered to him.

Ward walked over to him, drink in hand. They drank together for a while in silence, keeping their eyes trained on the dance floor. When the song ended and the DJ announced a fifteen-minute break, the hum of lively conversation and laughter reached their ears. Sophia made quiet work of seeing that everyone was accommodated and having a good time. The food had been served and things were going smoothly.

"Ruth is sure having a good time," Ward said. "Your father would have been pleased to see this."

For once, Logan had to agree about his father. He'd been a fair and decent employer—that much he would grant him, and he would have approved of honoring Ruth's service to Sunset Lodge like this. "She sure was surprised."

"You pulled it off," Ward said, taking a sip of whiskey.

"Not me so much. Sophia."

Logan's gaze landed on her again. She was never far from his scope of vision. He'd been deliberately watching her all night. Truth be told, even if he tried, he wouldn't be able to keep his eyes off her.

"She's a hard worker. Real nice, too," Ward said. "I think my boy is smitten."

Restrained laughter slipped from Logan's mouth. "Yeah. Him and all the rest of the crew. She's no different than her mother in that regard."

Ward shot Logan a sideways glance. "Maybe the two women should be judged on their own merits. Or better yet, maybe they shouldn't be judged at all."

Ward's little lecture was getting on his nerves. Sure the man had status on the ranch. He and his father had been close, and Ward looked upon the Slade boys as kin, but Logan wasn't going to change his mind about Sophia Montrose, no matter how many people came to her defense.

"Just being cautious, Ward."

"That why she's been in your line of vision all night?"

Logan eyed him with a sour look. "You keeping track?"

"I'm thinking you should go over there and ask her to dance when the music starts up again."

"And I'm thinking she's got no room on her dance card."

Ward let out a hearty laugh. "I bet she'd make room for you."

Logan shook his head slowly. "Doubtful. I'm the devil to her."

Ward finished off his drink and set it down on a nearby table. "Maybe you should stop acting like one. Give the lady a chance." With that, Ward walked toward his son and started up a conversation with him.

Logan frowned and marched over to the bar to get another drink.

Before dinner, Logan walked up the steps to the deck and offered up a toast and tribute to Ruth. Everyone stood and raised their glasses. His speech was short but filled with gratitude for her outstanding service, especially during these past

few trying months after his father's death. He managed to get
a few laughs with anecdotes about Ruth's first days on the
job and he wished her well in her retirement.

When the speech was over, Ruth was summoned up to say
a few words. Her heartfelt goodbye and vow to get even with
Logan for conning her with this surprise party brought some
misty-eyed laughter from the gathering.

After dinner, dessert and coffee were served, the music
mellowed out and one by one the guests began taking their
leave. Sophia walked many of them outside. Logan didn't
miss the way she stood on his doorstep with a proprietary
hand on the door as she thanked the guests for coming and
wished them a safe drive home. She said all the right things.
She was the perfect hostess.

Logan was just about to pay her the compliment when his
phone buzzed. It was late and he didn't want to take any calls
tonight but when the caller ID popped up on the screen, Logan
immediately answered the call from his youngest brother.

"Hey, Justin. How're the marines treating you these days?"

Logan walked into his office to speak with his brother
about when he was coming home. His brother loved the mil-
itary, but Logan sensed a longing for Sunset Ranch in him
lately. Twenty minutes later, when he strode to the backyard,
he found all the guests gone. The housekeeping staff was fold-
ing up the tablecloths, breaking down the tables and stacking the chairs. They were an efficient machine that didn't
need any help from him, so he pivoted and went in search
of Sophia.

"Where is Ms, Montrose?" he asked one of the waiters in
the kitchen.

"She left with Mrs. Polanski ten minutes ago," he said.
"She said to tell you good-night."

Logan waited until the last of his staff had cleaned up and
taken off before he plopped down on the sofa, letting go a
weary sigh. He knew how to pick good horseflesh. He knew

what stallions would produce the best offspring. He knew how to keep his farm running smoothly and in the black, but what he knew about throwing a surprise party would fit in a shot glass with room to spare.

Ruth had been pleased and had thanked him half a dozen times. Her service had been recognized. His father *would* have been proud of how it all went down.

His father.

Logan had idolized him. Growing up as the eldest son, he'd wanted to be just like Randall Slade one day: fair, decent, honest, hardworking. He'd thought the sun rose and set on that man's shoulders. Until one day, his faith in his father had been destroyed.

It was past midnight on a school night when Logan woke from a bad dream. Sweat beaded on his forehead and his body trembled as his eyes opened to the darkness of his bedroom. Too keyed up to sleep, Logan rose and knew what would calm him. Logan had gotten only a glimpse of him when he'd first arrived today. Champion, the purebred Arabian stallion.

Logan tiptoed out of the house to keep from waking his parents. His father would not approve of an unsupervised visit to a horse new to the farm. Stallions were known for erratic behavior, especially in new environments. So Logan was careful not to make a peep as he walked toward the barn and the special stall designated for Champion.

He'd gotten ten feet into the huge barn when he'd heard whispers in the dark.

How he'd wished he'd turned around and run home.

But instead, he'd hidden outside of the tack room and listened.

"I need you in my life, Louisa. You're the only woman I've ever loved."

It was his father's voice.

Panicked now, Logan couldn't move. Curiosity and disbelief kept him glued in place.

His father was talking to Louisa Montrose, the manager of Sunset Lodge.

"I love you, too, mi amor," Lousia whispered. "I want you with me always."

Logan's ears burned as he heard their soft sighs and passionate moans. It wasn't so dark that Logan couldn't peer through the slits in the wood and see his father sprawled over Louisa on the tack room cot, kissing her, making little sounds of pleasure whisper from her lips.

"You know why I married her, Louisa. It was a merger of our families' land," he said. "And she was pregnant with Logan."

"It doesn't matter," Louisa said on a breath. "It doesn't matter."

Logan snapped his eyes opened. Reliving that memory never brought him any peace. Why would it? That night, Logan had been shocked and felt a keen overwhelming sense of loss. Everything he'd believed about his life was a lie. His father had been a scoundrel. He'd married for business reasons. He'd married because he'd gotten a woman pregnant. With that notion came great heartache. Logan's birth had been an accident. They hadn't wanted him. But even more than that, the man Logan had come to love, admire and idolize wasn't who he thought him to be.

Logan had caught his father in the act of adultery fifty yards from where his mother slept.

Not a pretty sight for a boy on the threshold of manhood.

That memory put him on edge. Why in hell did Ward have to mention his father tonight? Logan rose from his seat and roamed aimlessly around the house. His restlessness unnerved him as the images of his father and Louisa Montrose played over and over in his mind.

He spotted Sophia's black-sequined wrap lying across the entryway table. She'd left the party without it. On impulse, he picked it up and brought it to his nose, taking in the exotic scent that was uniquely hers. Logan closed his eyes for a moment, savoring the fragrance. Then, without hesitation and with her wrap clutched in his hand, he strode out the front door.

Tonight, not even Logan's sharpest sense of warning could stop him from seeking Sophia out.

Sophia parked her car in the driveway and breathed a big sigh of relief. She was finally home. She'd had a long, tiring day and she was glad it was over. The party had gone as planned. Ruth's husband had driven the grandkids home and Sophia had offered to drop Ruth back off at her house. On the way, Ruth had gushed again at how much she'd appreciated the party and how grateful she was to Sophia for all the work she'd put into it.

Sophia appreciated being appreciated and she was also glad to have made a dear friend in Ruth. After this weekend, Sophia would be managing Sunset Lodge by herself. Luckily, as her friend had reminded her, Ruth was only a phone call away if she needed advice.

With her body dragging, Sophia exited her car. She was ready for a hot shower and a good night's sleep. She'd earned it this week.

Stepping from the pavement onto the flowery path toward her front door, she heard a noise. Footsteps crunching on spring leaves. She whipped around. Knotted in fear, she focused her attention on the source of the sound. It was coming from behind a row of pink azalea bushes on the side of the cottage. Straining her eyes to see beyond the porch lamp's circle of light, she couldn't make out anything in the dark. Her heart beat wildly. Crazy thoughts entered her head. She imagined someone darting out from the bushes to attack her.

A madman was after her. He'd followed her from Las Vegas. He knew her every move.

Sophia couldn't get inside the house fast enough. She fumbled with the key. It fell from her shaky hands and pinged onto the brick porch. "Oh, no."

She scrambled to pick it up and out of the corner of her eye she saw another movement, a tall shadow that crossed into the lamplit path from the opposite direction of the azalea bushes. Fear immobilized her as she struggled to make sense of it. Fleeting questions rushed through her mind. Were they coming at her from two different directions? Steeling her nerves, she vowed she wouldn't be a helpless victim. She whirled around, ready to take a swing, ready to defend herself, ready to scream. She opened her mouth, her arm raised for a fight.

"Sophia?" Logan's questioning voice broke through her panic. She saw his Stetson first, as he approached from out of the shadows and into the light.

A dire gasp of relief escaped her throat. "Logan?" Slowly, she slumped against the front door, her legs shaking so badly she could barely stand. The door did a good job of keeping her upright. "Thank God, it's you."

"You look white as a sheet," he said softly, as if she were a child. "What's got you so scared?"

Tears welled in her eyes. She put her hand to her mouth and shook her head.

"Did someone hurt you?"

She continued to shake her head. "I'm f-fine. I, uh… What are you doing here?"

He held out the sequined wrap she'd worn to the party. "You left this."

"I didn't hear your car pull up."

"I walked over."

Sophia didn't respond.

"You're shaking like a leaf." He took the key she was gripping for dear life out of her hand and inserted it into the lock. "Let's get you inside the house."

Sophia managed to step out of his way, and once he opened the door he put his hand to her back and guided her to the parlor sofa. "Have a seat."

Sophia obeyed him automatically. She was still trembling as she sank into the cushions. She closed her eyes and inhaled a quiet breath to calm down. She was safe. Logan was here. The cushions gave way when he took a seat on the opposite end of the sofa.

"What happened out there?"

Sophia snapped her eyes open at his serious tone. All softness was gone from his voice. Leaning forward with elbows braced on his knees, he turned his head to face her.

"I want the truth."

Despite her distracted mind, the insult registered. He believed that she was accustomed to lying to him and *this* time he demanded she speak with honesty. But she couldn't do battle with him tonight over his remark. She was comforted to have him here. "The *truth* is, I thought someone was out there. I heard a noise by the azaleas."

"Go on."

Sophia looked away from him.

"There's got to be more than that. You've lived on this ranch before. You know there's dozens of species of animals that could make noises in the bushes before scurrying away. When I arrived, you said, 'Thank God, it's you.' Has someone been bothering you?"

"Besides you?" She smiled sweetly but his frown said he didn't find any humor in her statement. "Sorry. I was actually relieved that you showed up when you did."

"Now I know something's wrong. You're never glad to see me. Tell me."

Sophia sighed. She didn't want to get into this with Logan, but her fear was very real tonight and judging by the look on his face, he wasn't going anywhere without an explanation. "I've received three notes on my doorstep," she began, and then recounted the incidents that had happened since she'd moved to the cottage. When Logan questioned her further, Sophia had no choice but to explain about the similar incidents in Las Vegas.

Logan sat quietly listening to her, asking a probing question here and there, and once all was out in the open about her would-be Fantasy Follies stalker, Logan made an announcement. "We need to go to the sheriff."

"No," Sophia said. "I won't do that."

"Why the hell not?"

"I've been through this before. The notes aren't threatening and there's nothing they can do anyway. And…I don't want to bring negative attention to Sunset Lodge. Monday is my first day as a full-fledged manager."

"You were scared out of your mind a minute ago."

"It could be nothing. I have a secret admirer, maybe." Sophia was grasping at straws.

"I'm sure you have more than a few of those, but if someone is putting notes on your doorstep and *watching* you…you don't want to mess with that."

"I don't know that for sure. Maybe my imagination got the best of me. Maybe it was a wild animal in the bushes."

"You don't believe that," Logan said, "and now I don't, either. Not after hearing about the notes. Are you refusing to speak with the sheriff?"

She gave him a nod. "Yes, I am refusing."

Logan's eyes narrowed on her, but she wasn't going to back down. She'd had enough bad press and negative attention when she married Gordon Gregory. She didn't want a media circus here at Sunset Lodge. It was a place of serenity and beauty. She wouldn't mar that perception with the law snooping around, questioning staff and guests. She loved Sunset Lodge too much for that.

Logan rubbed his jaw as he considered her from across the sofa. "You know we have a good security system on the ranch and at the lodge. Now I'm thinking that might have been breached. Someone on the ranch may be out for no good. That makes it my business, Sophia. And, frankly, it worries me. You won't go to the law, and I can't have you living here alone anymore."

"Meaning what?" Sophia didn't like the way he was steering this conversation.

"Meaning, you're moving into the main house with me. And it's not up for discussion."

Seven

Every bone in her body was well aware that she was living alone with Logan Slade. The house was big, but not big enough to miss seeing him saunter into the kitchen in the morning with an unshaven face and sexy, mussed hair. Or notice him unbutton his shirt, exposing a sliver of bronzed skin as he headed to his bedroom for a shower. With Luke gone, Sophia didn't have the buffer she needed to keep up the facade that somehow Logan hadn't begun to wedge his way into her heart.

He checked in on her in the morning at breakfast and insisted that she have dinner at the house every night. When Sophia's eyes would light up over his concern, his expression would turn to stone and he'd remind her that safety on the ranch was the key issue.

Sophia should have been exhausted. Putting in long hours at the lodge during the day was enough to fatigue an Olympic athlete, much less a woman of her size and stature. But the truth was, Sophia had restless energy. Seeing Logan coming in and out of the house every day, made her jumpy and anxious. They'd have brief, stilted conversations at meals, and before he rose from the table, Logan would gaze at her with yearning in his eyes. It was fleeting and reluctant, but Sophia saw it. He wasn't as immune to her as he let on. Maybe the wall of defense he'd built up against her was beginning to crumble a little bit.

Now, three days into her stay at his home, Sophia watched him rise from the dinner table as usual, the moment the last bite on his plate was gone. "I'm going to turn in early," he said, stretching his arms over his head. He looked a little weary with a five-o'clock shadow on his face and reddened eyes.

Sophia nodded. "Good night," she said politely, then blurted what was on her mind. "I think I'll take a ride."

"Where? The stores will be closing soon."

Sophia smiled. "Not that kind of ride. I'm not interested in shopping. I need some air. I thought I'd ask Hunter to saddle up a mare and ride out with me."

"I sent Hunter home an hour ago."

Sophia shrugged a shoulder. "That's okay. I'll find someone else." Sophia rose from the table, grabbing his empty plate along with hers.

He reached out to touch her upper arm. "Just about everyone's gone home for the night. Why don't you turn in and do it another time?"

"I'm not a prisoner here, am I? I can saddle up a horse and take a ride."

His hand wound around her arm, gently, but only to make his point. "It'll be dark in less than an hour, Sophia."

His penetrating gaze bored into her and they stared at each other for a long while. Finally, he released his hold on her. "Fine, suit yourself."

Sophia didn't get any satisfaction in upsetting Logan. She didn't set out to annoy him, but she did need an outlet for her pent-up energy. And a ride along the paths of Sunset Ranch would do the trick. She wasn't fool enough to go by herself. She should be able to find a riding partner, if not here at the ranch, then at the lodge.

Twenty minutes later, after changing into her riding clothes, Sophia walked into the barn. Horses whinnied in their stalls. Some kicked and others brought their heads up to greet her with a snort as she walked by. She stopped to stroke the face of a good-natured aging palomino. "Hello, Buttercup."

Buttercup wasn't a star of pure-breeding stock that would be sold off to clients. She and half a dozen other horses were kept on the premises to take prospective clients for rides in the pasture and, more important, to lend a mellow tone to the more spirited animals in the barn.

Sophia gave each of the horses a little attention as she headed to the tack room to pick up her gear. There wasn't a soul around to help her saddle up and just as she was going to take Logan's advice and turn back, changing her mind about the ride, he appeared in the doorway.

"You still want that ride?" he asked.

Startled by his appearance, Sophia tamped down her initial gut reaction. But Logan noticed the momentary fear she couldn't hide from her expression. "Oh, uh…yes. I'd like to take a ride."

"You're still jumpy, aren't you?"

"No."

The sound of his boots echoed against the walls as he strode farther into the small room until his face was inches from hers. "You are."

"Not now. I have you here. And there haven't been any more notes or incidents."

"You knew I wouldn't let you take a ride alone. Or go with anyone else."

Sophia stared at him. "Is that what you thought? I was hinting for you to take me?"

"Weren't you?"

"No, I just wanted to get out of the house."

"I'd think you'd want some peace after working all day."

"The house is…"

"Is what, Sophia?" Logan whispered her name.

"Lonely," she said, confessing one of her vulnerabilities.

His expression changed, softened. His gaze traveled up and down her body until she was so excited that her breathing grew ragged and heavy. Her chest heaving now, Logan stared at the top button on her blouse that prevented her breasts from spilling out.

"Without Luke in the house, and you barely speaking to me—"

"Luke?" Something flickered in his eyes. "You don't want Luke."

Sophia's heart raced. The conversation had switched direction. And Logan's powerful gaze destroyed her rational sense. "Luke's my fri—"

Logan pulled her into his arms. He smelled of earth and musk, so strong, so powerful. His breath warmed her throat and his words made her mouth go dry. "We're not gonna talk about my brother tonight, darlin'."

His determination made her go limp. Her voice lowered until she could barely hear the words she spoke, "Wh-what are we going to talk about?"

He brought her body tight against his. "Your loneliness." Then he smiled, a flash against a stark, handsome face, the gleam brightening his eyes. "Then again, we don't have to do much talking at all."

His lips touched hers tenderly as if he wanted to draw out all of her fears, all of her loneliness. The kiss was sweetly gentle, and Sophia had to remind herself that it was Logan who was kissing her, Logan who held her in his arms.

He brought his hands to her face and cupped her cheeks, murmuring sweet nothings as he kissed her. Sophia surrendered herself to the compassion Logan was showing her. He suckled her lips, tasting from her, his firm delicious mouth giving her time to adjust to what was happening between them. "You're safe with me," he whispered over her lips.

She felt protected and cared for but then in the back of her mind, coming from a very dark place, a warning bell sounded.

This was Logan Slade. He hated her.

So why did he make her feel as if she were floating on a cloud?

She ignored her misgivings and dove into the sensations he stirred in her. She'd always been attracted to Logan and now, with his kisses heating her through and through, she thought she could be a little bit in love with him. She told herself that and stopped trying to analyze the pleasure he offered her. It felt too good having him strip away her loneliness.

Sophia placed her hands on his chest, her fingers spreading across rough cotton as she stroked him eagerly. A groan emanated from his throat and Sophia continued to touch him, to explore the strong washboard across his ribs.

He slipped off her ponytail holder and in the faint, fading sunlight watched her hair flow freely to frame her face. Appreciation shone in the glint of his eyes and he released a relenting sound that came from the depths of his throat. "You make me forget who I am," he murmured.

Sophia put her arms around his neck and rose up to kiss him soundly on the lips. Softly, she whispered, "You're Logan Slade and you don't like me very much."

Logan wove his hands through her long hair, letting the tresses slip between his fingers. He released a deep sigh. "There are things I like about you, Sophia. More than I've liked about any other woman."

He pressed his mouth to hers again. Sophia relished the kiss and the words behind the kiss. She whispered over his lips, "What do you like about me?"

"Kissing you is right up there," he said softly.

He paused to gaze at the strands of hair framing her face. "You've got the prettiest hair."

A soft whimper escaped her throat. His compliments were a heady elixir.

He slid his hands over her shoulders and stroked down her arms. Tingles erupted from his soft caress. "Your body is perfect. It's been killing me living with you. Knowing you're lying just steps away in another bedroom."

Fiery heat arrowed down her belly. "Logan," she breathed out.

There was no stopping this now. They were caught up in a game that had only one outcome. He pulled her taut against his rock-hard chest. Jeans to jeans, their legs touched, denim rubbing together. His hand rested on the soft material of her white blouse and with two nimble fingers he stroked her exposed skin just above the buttons.

Sophia's breath caught. She closed her eyes, savoring the sensual touch that brought goose bumps. He toyed with her there, making her ache, making her lean back and give him reign to do what he pleased.

She heard a snap and then a tear as her blouse split apart, two buttons flying onto the floor. Her eyes popped open. He watched her, waited for her approval.

She smiled and a little bubble of laughter rose from her throat.

Logan pulled the blouse out of her jeans and off her shoulders, discarding it with a flick of his wrist. Then he touched the top of her breasts, the flat of his palms against her plump ripe skin spilling from her bra. "I like touching you. I can't get enough."

He unhooked her bra and with a reverent groan watched her breasts fall free of their restraints. The look on his face made her body ache for more. He cupped her, weighed the globes in his hands as he kissed her again and again. Their mouths opened and the kisses grew hotter and more frenzied.

After a minute, Logan slid his lips to her ear, his words clipped and ragged. "In another second, I'm not gonna be able to stop."

Sophia understood him. She was already at the point of no return. But Logan wasn't a brute—he gave her the choice.

"I don't want you to."

"Don't move," he said.

And she stood there, waiting while Logan set a quilt on a weathered leather sofa that was banked against the tack room wall. He came back to lift her into his arms, and then lowered her down gently. He removed her boots and the rest of her clothes.

Then he stared at her for a few seconds.

She felt exposed. Naked and lying in wait for him to make love to her.

"I like the way your eyes darken when you look at me," he said, and then added, "I knew you were beautiful, but Sophia, honey, you take my breath away."

And suddenly she didn't feel ashamed or embarrassed anymore. She didn't feel vulnerable. She wanted this. She wanted Logan. There wasn't a doubt in her mind.

Next, he removed his shirt and a glow lit her eyes when everything else came off.

"Mercy," Sophia uttered, gazing at him.

"I'll take that as a compliment, darlin'."

But Logan didn't cover her with his body right away. Instead he came up beside her to kiss her again. "Close your eyes," he ordered.

She obeyed.

His touch was soft and gentle as he stroked her between her thighs. And when his ministrations grew more bold, more forceful, she shuddered and let go a tiny moan of pleasure. Logan was relentless and worked her body, tormenting her until her moans were continuous and in tune with the throbbing heat pulsating at her core.

Her body jerked and splintered. Her breaths short and quick, she experienced a powerful release.

"Sophia," Logan murmured, as she came down to earth. Gently, he stroked her hair and kissed her cheeks. "You have no idea what a turn-on it is seeing you go wild like that."

The room was darker now. The sun had almost set and Sophia could barely make out Logan's shadow as he brought himself down on top of her. She reached out, desperately wanting to be joined with him.

He spoke with urgency, his voice a rasp that thrilled her. "I've waited a long time for this. For you."

Twenty minutes later, cocooned in the warmth of Logan's strong arms, Sophia opened her eyes to darkness. The air inside the tack room was Nevada-dry and cool yet both of their bodies glistened with hot, sticky sweat.

Sophia sighed at the completion she felt. A soft purr hummed through her body. Every ounce of her flesh felt pleasantly devoured. Logan was an expert lover and he'd brought out her wilder side with his whispered words of encouragement, his powerful thrusts and his strong body covering hers.

Their releases had come out of sync with each other, but Sophia hadn't minded. She liked going first. Then she watched Logan's face twist with pleasure as he groaned from his inner depths until one last potent plunge brought him over the edge.

After that, they'd both fallen in a heap of exhaustion.

Quietly stunned.

And when Sophia's thoughts traveled once again to that dark place of uncertainty, Logan was there, stroking her arm and kissing her forehead. She relished his touch and the soothing way he treated her in the aftermath of lovemaking. The few lovers she'd had before hadn't been nearly as attentive after the deed was done. Sophia had made mistakes with men, but she'd never kept a man around if he wasn't respectful.

Where would she and Logan go from here? She had no idea what he was thinking. He'd said all the right things. He'd *done* all the right things and her body sang from the sweetest pleasure a man could give a woman. Now Sophia was at a crossroads in her life.

She'd been wary of Logan Slade for as long as she could remember. Tonight, she'd let down her guard and allowed him entrance not only to her body, but to her heart.

She loved Logan.

She was sure of it now.

She couldn't have given to him what she'd denied even the most persuasive of men who had come in and out of her life, without feeling great emotion. She'd given him her trust and hadn't regretted it for a second.

"How you doing, darlin'?"

The endearments he'd been using with her tonight made her smile inside. She assumed that he thought of her as a brat, a bitch and a hussy so to hear him come full circle gave her joy. "I'm pretty good."

"I won't argue there." He turned on his side to face her and she curled around to look him in the eyes. "You cold?" he asked.

"A little bit."

He slid his hand up and down along the curve of her hip, and each inch of naked skin warmed under his touch. "We should probably get out of here. Someone might walk in."

Sophia's eyes rounded. She hadn't thought of that. She'd lost all sense of time and place when Logan had seduced her. "We probably should."

Logan gave her a reluctant look, and then rose first. In the dark, he found her clothes strewn across the floor and handed them to her. She sat up to put them on and watched him in the shadows, a sense of pride swelling in her heart. How could she feel this way about a man who had injured her so often?

Once they were dressed—Sophia had a dickens of a time securing her blouse without the buttons, so Logan gave her his shirt to put on—they walked quietly out of the room and through the barn. Horses whinnied and snickered as they strode by, but they didn't take the time to give them attention. When they reached the wide double doors, Logan peered out, looking right, then left.

"Do you think someone's out there?" she asked, not worried about her would-be stalker so much as an employee wandering the grounds and catching them half dressed.

"Don't know."

"Should we walk out separately?"

Logan grinned and shook his head. "Honey, you moved into my house three days ago. You think any man on my ranch is thinking we're baking cookies inside?"

Sophia's brows lifted. "But that's not true! We weren't doing anything."

His grin slipped into a small smile. He gazed out the barn door again. "Not up until about an hour ago. Doesn't matter now. You want to make a run for it?" He put out his hand and stared at her.

Sophia saw the adventure in that. They had to travel the length of half a football field to make it to the house. She tucked her hand in his and they made a mad dash across the yard.

Sophia's soft laughter bubbled over. She hadn't felt this carefree in years. She ran a step behind Logan, who tugged her along, and she could have sworn she heard the beautiful sound of his laughter, too.

Tonight, Logan wanted dessert. And he wanted Sophia. The two went hand in hand in his mind. Both would satisfy his craving. "Let's have some ice cream," he said as they came to a halt inside his house.

Sophia's topaz eyes brilliant and her breaths labored, she smiled at him as if he were a child. "Let me guess. You want strawberry?"

He blinked. "How did you know?"

"It's your favorite. I remember from birthday parties here. I like vanilla, Luke likes chocolate and you love strawberry."

"Observant. Add that to the list of things I like about Sophia Montrose. Come on," he said, stifling his frustration. He wouldn't let the fact that Sophia always had Luke's name on her lips bother him tonight. His brother was a part of their equation and he always had been. Luke and Sophia were friends, and he would make sure that's all they ever would be.

Luke had a weak spot when it came to Sophia.

Logan wouldn't be so naive.

He hadn't meant to bed Sophia but now that he had, he wasn't fool enough to let her go until he was good and ready. No man in his right mind would let a luscious beauty like Sophia slip through his fingers. But he still didn't trust her motives. He knew enough to be wary of her, even as he held her hand in his as he led her to the kitchen. "C'mon. I'm sure we can scrounge up some vanilla ice cream for you."

Dressed in his shirt that was three sizes too big for her, her hair wild about her face, Sophia followed him into the kitchen. Moonlight streamed in through a window and the wide, double-paneled back door. Logan decided to keep the lights off. He liked seeing Sophia by the light of the moon. "Have a seat while I dish it up." He pulled out a stool for her behind the rectangular island countertop and she sat down.

"Logan Slade serving me?" She leaned forward, bracing her elbows on the granite with her fists under her chin. "Hell *must* have frozen over."

He grinned. "It's a night for firsts. The fat lady sang *and* pigs flew in the barn a few minutes ago."

Immediate color rushed to her face, painting her olive skin rosy. "Maybe there is such a thing as miracles."

Logan opened the freezer door with a big smile on his face. Sparring with Sophia kept him on his toes. "It was sorta like an out-of-body experience, honey."

"Yes. Who would have believed?"

"Not me and sure as anything, not you, I'd venture to guess."

"I wanted a ride."

Logan brought out two half gallons of ice cream and set them on the counter in front of her. Wiggling his eyebrows, he said, "Be careful what you wish for."

"I'll try to remember that."

He came up with a scoop and began dishing vanilla and strawberry ice cream into two bowls. He slid one over to her.

"Are we going to eat this in the dark?" she asked.

"You mind?"

She thought about it a moment and then shook her head. "Not at all, but why?"

"Things taste better in the dark."

"Really?"

"Think about it…what do you do when you really want to savor something?"

Sophia's lips curved up. "You close your eyes."

"Exactly."

She nodded. "I never thought about it, but it makes sense."

Logan plopped down on the stool next to her and dove into his ice cream, taking a big bite. Then he closed his eyes. Strawberry ice cream and Sophia all in one night *was* something to savor. He didn't know what compelled him to divulge the truth, but before he could hold it back, he blurted, "Until a second ago, I didn't know that, either. The honest truth is that you look dazzling in moonlight and I couldn't see spoiling the mood with artificial lighting. The other stuff I said is a load of horse manure."

Sophia put her head down, her eyes downcast. She stared at her ice cream then began shaking her head. Logan wasn't sure what to make of it—he'd never admitted to feeding baloney to anyone before.

When Sophia finally lifted her head, amusement lit her eyes and she laughed right in his face, giggling so hard she put her spoon down to contain the laughter with a hand to the stomach.

"What? I pay you a compliment and you laugh." Logan's ears rang from the contagious sound of her sweet giggles. He spooned another chunk of ice cream into his mouth and swallowed, unable to keep from grinning along with her.

"Oh, Logan," she said between chuckles, "you always amaze me."

It seemed to be a night of amazements. He jammed another spoonful of ice cream into his mouth and then pointed to her bowl scooped high with vanilla ice cream. "Eat up, darlin'. You're lagging."

She dipped her spoon in and gave it a taste. Her dark-lashed eyes slowly closed as she swallowed. A lump formed in Logan's throat. Watching Sophia relish anything was like watching an artist apply the first strokes of paint to a fresh canvas.

And tonight, Sophia had been hard to resist. Besides her beautiful face and knockout body, she made him smile. They'd had incredible sex less than an hour ago. Why shouldn't he laugh along with her and allow himself a night of indulgence?

"Here," he said after watching Sophia take two more delicate bites of her ice cream. "Let me help."

He took the spoon from her hand and scooped up a good-sized amount of vanilla ice cream from the bowl. Sophia's lips eagerly parted for him with a sensual curve upward as he inserted the spoon into her mouth. This wasn't like feeding a baby, Logan mused. It was erotic as hell. Her mouth moved up and down and her eyelids closed as she tasted the dessert he fed her. He leaned closer, whispering, "I want more, Sophia."

Her eyes snapped open and without hesitation, she replied softly, "So do I."

Logan brought his mouth to hers, brushing a gentle kiss over her chilled lips. He tasted the sweet vanilla cream that lingered there. "I'm not talking about ice cream."

She nodded and whispered, "I'm not hungry for ice cream, either."

Logan's heart hammered in his chest. The woman was a temptation that could destroy a weaker man. Logan pushed his seat out and stood, taking Sophia by her arms and lifting her up against him. She wrapped both arms around his neck and he bent his head to take her in a fiery kiss that got all of his juices flowing. He pulled her closer, melding their bodies, fitting her against him like a tailor-made suit. He curved his hands on the slope of her buttocks and rocked her against the erection straining his jeans.

Sophia moaned at the deliberate contact, giving him a little cry of anticipation that matched his own desperate desire.

He swept her up and carried her out of the kitchen and down the long hallway. Her eyes gleaming, her body nearly weightless in his arms, he kissed her several times as he strode into his master bedroom. When he reached his large bed, he turned down his bedspread and then lowered Sophia onto silky sheets. Her luxurious hair fanned out against the pillow and he stripped her bare within seconds, needing to see her naked on his bed.

His fantasies, the secret ones he'd kept hidden from the world, came to fruition, seeing her here now, waiting for him with lust in her eyes. He'd bedded her once tonight, quickly, on a worn-out sofa in the barn, but this was where Sophia needed to be. Cast in moonlight, her body accommodated on a luxurious bed—his bed—and now Logan would take his time with her. He would savor her like she was a sweet bowl of strawberry ice cream. And he would lick every last creamy inch of her, until they were both satisfied.

"As much as I like you in my shirt, taking it off is definitely an improvement."

Sophia wasn't coy or timid; she was bold as she lay there allowing him to study her. She was a rare find, a woman who could easily grace the cover of the *Sports Illustrated* swimsuit issue. She was perfect in her naked form.

"I'm a little lonely in this big bed," she whispered, rolling to her side and patting the area next to her.

"I told you I'd take care of your loneliness."

He unhooked his belt, kicked off his boots and then lowered himself down onto the bed. He reached for her, just as she came up over him to straddle his thighs. He'd kept his jeans on, and now he wished he hadn't.

"You're lonely, too, Logan," she said softly. "You simply don't realize it."

There was truth to that, he admitted to himself, but now was not the time for that conversation. "Then keep me company for a while."

"I intend to," she whispered.

Her breasts were round and full, overflowing in his hands. A man could die happy like this. He brought one rosy-tipped peak into his mouth and Sophia uttered a little cry of pleasure. Logan paid proper attention to both of her breasts, cupping and weighing them, kissing and suckling. Sophia was lost, writhing with uncontrolled passion.

She was beautiful atop him. Her hands flat on his chest, her body fluid and primed for sex, Logan's control was ready to snap. It was too much and not enough. He wanted to own her, to take possession and never let go. It was strange to feel that way about any woman, but with Sophia it felt right.

He made love to every ounce of her with heated kisses and strokes of his tongue until he could barely breathe from the fire building in his system. His hands wove through her long thick hair and he bruised her lips with hot crushing kisses.

He made sure Sophia was well loved in every way. It pleased him to please her.

His mind briefly went to his father and how he'd lusted after Louisa Montrose. The only difference being that Logan wasn't married to another woman. He hadn't spoken vows or pledged his love to one woman and then bedded another. He would never fall in love with a Montrose. Sophia wouldn't break him. Not in that way.

He wanted her in his bed.

He'd never fall into the same trap his father had.

Nothing had changed in that regard.

Sophia's soft, labored moans were frantic. She unzipped his jeans, and all thoughts of his father went out the window. The gorgeous woman slipped her hand around his swollen member and he'd barely had time to put a condom on before she sought an end to their mutual torment.

He guided her down and with one slow, earth-shattering thrust they were joined.

Sophia tossed her head back, taking him inside her. The arch of her back, the sheet of dark hair tossing from side to side as she slid her sweet body over his, were a thing of beauty.

Logan seared those images into his memory as they rode the waves of glory together.

I love you, Logan, Sophia thought as she glanced at him. Though he was normally well-groomed, this morning, short, thick strands of his hair stuck out in several directions and a day-old beard darkened his handsome features.

Sophia wasn't going to cry. She wasn't going to make a scene. She would be strong. Like her mother. She wouldn't let Logan know how much she loved him. Not now. She couldn't trust him with those feelings. She couldn't tell him truths that he wasn't ready to hear. She knew it would take time, but Sophia had never been in love before. She'd never felt the full force of the emotion and the power it wielded might cause her great injury. She knew she would have to step carefully to avoid the land mines of her own making.

Sophia lay there with a lump in her throat. Logan had made love to her thoroughly last night. She still ached in private places from his ruthless pursuit of satisfying her. He had made his mark on her. She would never forget her first night with Logan Slade. She hoped there were many more to come. She would not give up on her love.

Was she being a fool?

Her mother's words rang out clearly in Sophia's mind. She had never forgotten them. "Loving Randall Slade was a waste of love."

Because it had ended in heartache. Sophia wouldn't allow that to happen with Logan. Her love would not be wasted. It couldn't be. She'd given everything she'd had to give to him. Would he be so cruel as to throw it all away?

Dawn peeked out on the horizon, the first glimmering rays of light sneaking into the room. Sophia gave Logan one last glance, and then rose from the bed. Her feet landed quietly on the floor and she tiptoed away hoping not to wake him.

She grabbed Logan's shirt she'd worn last night, along with her pants, and dressed before she exited the room. The Slades' household staff did not live at the house, but they would arrive shortly.

Logan's remark about how his men knew they weren't just baking cookies together came to mind.

Sophia cringed at the notion. She'd never wanted a reputation as a gold-digger, but it seemed to follow her every move. She would have fallen in love with Logan Slade even if he were penniless. Money wasn't the issue but who would believe that about her now? On paper, and from what people perceived about her, she appeared guilty.

And then there was Luke. What was she going to say to

him? When he arrived home, would he understand her motives? Would he hate that she'd fallen in love with his brother?

Sophia entered her room, quietly shutting the door behind her. She wasn't ready to start the day, but doubted she could fall back to sleep. She stripped off her clothes, walked into the bathroom and turned on the shower faucet. She stepped inside and let the warm water slide over her skin. She stood there for a long time in the steamy hot spray, deep in thought.

The night she shared with Logan had been remarkable. The earth had moved and the stars had aligned. She sighed at the memories—the taste of his mouth, the scratch of his stubble bruising her skin, his strong hands gentle on her, all rushed through her mind. It had been ecstasy and Sophia wouldn't allow herself to think of it as a one-night stand.

But she had no clue what Logan was thinking. She wondered if he'd set out to seduce her or if they'd been caught up in something powerful that both of them couldn't deny. Last night, their relationship had changed forever.

Sophia washed her hair and scrubbed her body with lavender-scented soap. The pleasing fragrance had always soothed her nerves and made her feel better. When she stepped out of the shower and dried off, most of her pressing doubts were banished.

Someone knocked on her bedroom door. Sophia took a quick breath, wrapped herself in a plush towel and shook out her wet hair before going to the door. "Who is it?"

"It's me, Sophia."

The sound of Logan's voice gave her tingles. She opened the door slowly. His cool dark eyes blazed with warmth when he looked at her draped in the towel. "Tempting."

He was dressed in business clothes, dark slacks and a white shirt. Seeing him again took her breath away. "Good morning."

"Mornin'. You're up early," he said.

"I, uh, woke up and couldn't fall back to sleep."

"You wanted to skip out of my room before the house-keeper arrived."

"Yes," she admitted, her face flaming. "Do you blame me?"

His smile was seductive, his voice a rasp of desire. "Don't run away from me, Sophia."

She nibbled on her lower lip, unsure what to say.

He stepped into the room with a gleam in his eyes. He reached for the top of her towel. Her throat tightened and she just stood there rooted to the spot with his big hand on her chest. When she thought he'd undo the towel, his fingers stayed on her skin just above the cotton. The intimate touch made goose bumps erupt on her arms.

He bent his head and kissed her, whispering over her lips, "You know I have a shower in my room. Big enough for two. Next time, we'll do it together."

An immediate image rushed into her mind and Logan smiled knowingly. But his automatic assumption that there would be a next time flashed in her head like a lightbulb moment.

Sophia surprised herself by saying, "We can't…" She hesitated, knowing in her heart this was the right thing to say. Even so, it pained her to draw a line in the sand. "We can't have an affair."

Logan didn't flinch, but she noted a quick flicker in his eyes. "Because we don't like each other?"

Because I've fallen in love with you and need more than that.

But Sophia couldn't tell him that. She couldn't trust him with her love. He was still the same man, with the same prejudices and opinions. "I never said I didn't like you."

The corner of his mouth crooked up. "Last night was good, Sophia. You can't deny it." He brushed her hair to one side, touching her shoulder in a soft caress. She trembled from his touch and the blazing warmth in his eyes. "We could have more nights like the one we just had."

She summoned her courage and asked him the question that would define this new relationship. "Have you changed your mind about my mother? About me? Do you still resent me and my presence here?"

The warmth in his eyes evaporated. He dropped his hand from her hair. "Don't go there, Sophia. It'll only ruin things."

Sophia closed her eyes. She had her answer and her heart ached with the brutal truth. Last night hadn't been about fondness, caring or love. It had been about lust and sex. Logan didn't have to say the words, but she knew now that she'd been a fool to think he'd change his mind so easily. He still thought her mother was a calculating home wrecker. He'd probably thought worse of Sophia. He still took exception to her inheritance. She couldn't forget that he'd tried to buy out her share of Sunset Lodge when she'd first arrived just to get rid of her.

Yet her love for him didn't diminish. It didn't fade, not even a tiny bit, knowing what he thought about her. Sophia loved him from the bottom of her heart. And unfortunately, it would take a lot more heartache before she stopped loving him. But she wouldn't give any more of herself until he could make her believe there was some hope.

She tilted her chin, thinking haughtiness worked better with clothes on, but a towel and wet hair would have to do in this circumstance. "Then we have nothing to talk about."

Boldly, she searched his eyes, daring him to say something. To plead his case or try to convince her otherwise. But Logan didn't say a word.

Instead, he reached out and slowly unwrapped the towel from around her body. The material dropped to the floor in a lush heap. She stood bared to him, her skin freshly cleaned and perfumed.

He raked his gaze over her naked form and then inhaled

a sharp clipped breath. His mouth moved and she listened to words that would stay with her until the end of time. "This isn't over, Sophia. You'll see that soon enough."

Eight

Sophia sat in the office she no longer shared with Ruth Polanski, her desk the only one in the room now. She'd turned it around to face the window and the verdant grounds of the lodge with the regal Sierra Nevada Mountains in the background. She could be happy here. No, she amended that. She *would* be happy here. Living a peaceful life at Sunset Ranch was what she truly wanted now.

All of the managerial duties at Sunset Lodge were on her shoulders. She relished the challenge, and dove into her work. This morning she had to make phone calls to vendors and deal with a stable boy who'd been rude to one of the guests. In the afternoon, she had a luncheon planned with a local landscaper. Sophia had a few changes in mind that would enhance the overall property. And she had to go over Logan's budget for the year.

She heard footsteps approaching, and turned to find Hunter Halliday standing behind her half-closed door. In his arms, he held an exquisite arrangement of lilies. "Ms. Montrose?"

Technically, she was Mrs. Gregory, but she'd never used her legal name. She wondered what prompted her to think about that now. "Come in, Hunter."

The strapping boy sauntered into the room and stood in front of her desk, looking uncomfortable with the feminine flowers in his hands. Sophia stared at the stargazers tinted with a touch of pink on the petals. "They are lovely," she said when Hunter didn't volunteer any information.

He'd been staring at her.

"Oh, um… Mr. Slade sent me over with these."

"They're from Mr. Slade?" Sophia's mouth dropped open. For an instant, when she'd seen Hunter bringing them in, she'd thought the flowers had come from Hanson Landscapers. It wasn't unusual for vendors to send managers perks, thank-yous or deal sweeteners to butter them up.

"Yes, ma'am. And he said to read the note in *private*."

She felt her face turning three shades of pink. "Okay."

A small white envelope appeared in her line of vision as Hunter set the flowers down on the only cleared-off space on her desk. "All right to put these here?"

"Uh, yes. That's fine." The arrival of these amazingly beautiful flowers put a major roadblock in thinking that she could ignore what had happened between her and Logan last night.

This isn't over.

Those three words Logan had spoken echoed in her heart. She didn't want it to be over between her and Logan, either. Heavens, it had barely just begun. But Sophia's pride wasn't a small thing. She couldn't face herself in the mirror every morning, knowing that Logan hadn't changed his mind about her. How could she possibly give herself to him, love or no love, without expecting him to make some concessions, without him willing to hear her explanations and tell her side of the story?

He still thought of her mother as a wicked woman, and thought of her as a gold-digger.

She sighed aloud and Hunter's eyes snapped to hers. "Oh, uh, thanks for delivering the flowers, Hunter."

"You're welcome."

Hunter didn't budge an inch. He hovered by her desk, watching her.

She smiled.

He sent her a troubled look. There seemed to be something on the boy's mind.

"Is there anything else?" she asked.

"Yep. But I don't know if it's appropriate for me to say."

Sophia wanted to reassure the boy. His unease was practically tangible. "If something's bothering you, you can tell me what it is. Why don't you sit down?"

"Okay." He took a seat across the desk and didn't look any more comfortable in it than he did while he was standing. He rubbed his hands back and forth and Sophia waited for him to speak.

"It's about Gabriel Strongbow."

Sophia's brow rose at the name. He was the stable boy Sophia had received a complaint about. "What about him?"

"I guess you could say we're friends. I'd like to put in a good word for him, ma'am. If I might."

"I haven't spoken to him yet. But I'll listen to what he has to say."

"He thinks he's gonna be fired, and he really can't afford it. He's helping his mother out by working this job and trying to stay in school. And I just want to say that he wasn't rude to the guest."

"So, you're vouching for him?"

"Well, I wasn't there actually. But I've seen Gabe with Rebecca Wagner and he's been nice and polite to her. Rebecca has been flirting with him all week. They like each other is all. Rebecca handed him her phone number yesterday and

Mrs. Wagner found out about it and accused him of all sorts of things. Gabe hasn't done anything wrong."

Sophia knew of the Wagner family. Rebecca was a pretty sixteen-year-old girl. Ruth had told her the three Wagners were regulars at the lodge. They'd been coming twice a year for over a decade. "Sounds like Mrs. Wagner is overprotective of her daughter. But you know that we have strict rules about employees and guests. It's not a line but a wall that we've constructed at Sunset Lodge and it isn't to be breached."

"Yes, I know." Hunter took a deep breath. "Just had to say my piece."

"And I've heard you." Sophia sent him a smile. "You're a good friend to Gabe."

"Just want what's fair."

"I'll be fair with him," she said.

Hunter relaxed somewhat, his eyes filled with appreciation. "Thanks."

Sophia braced her arms on the desk and leaned forward. "Tell me about Gabriel Strongbow."

Hunter shrugged and contemplated briefly before he began. "He's a senior in high school. Working at the stables part-time. He's got a little sister. His dad passed about three years ago and now they're struggling to hang on to their house."

"I see." Sophia could relate to living from paycheck to paycheck, trying to keep from drowning in a sea of debt and hoping that her fate wasn't solely based on the whim of an employer. "Well, Gabe's been with us for over a year and up until this point," she said, fanning through the boy's file, "he's been a good employee. That's all I can tell you, Hunter. I really shouldn't have discussed this with you at all, so please keep this conversation to yourself."

"Yes, ma'am."

Hunter rose, gave her one last parting look and then took his leave.

Sophia got up and walked to the door, closing it while deep

in thought. Sometimes a manager had to be judge and jury. She had to determine what was best for the establishment without infringing on the employee's rights. It was a balancing act, but in this case unless the complaints proved true and there was a blatant miscarriage of rules, she was pretty sure Gabriel Strongbow's job wouldn't be in jeopardy.

Sophia had never fired anyone in her life.

Putting those thoughts aside, she walked over to the lily arrangement and stared at the flowers a moment. They were truly perfect. Logan couldn't have picked anything she would have liked more. It was uncanny how sometimes the two of them were on the same wavelength. Then there were the *other* times when they butted heads and saw things very differently.

Sophia braced herself. She didn't know what to expect from Logan Slade anymore but she was dying of curiosity to see what Logan had to say that was to be read in private. She lifted the white envelope from its plastic holder and slipped the small piece of paper out. Unfolding it, she read the handwritten note silently.

> *Sophia,*
> *Can't get the image of how I left you this morning out of my head.*
> *Have dinner with me tonight. 8:00 p.m.*
> *It'll be our first date.*
> *Change my mind.*
> *Logan*

Sophia's hand shook so much, the words she'd just read and then reread became fuzzy. She moved on wobbly legs to her chair and lowered down slowly, her fingers gripping the edges for balance. The world seemed to tilt off-kilter at the moment. She couldn't believe what Logan had written. He told her in those few sentences that he was willing to try.

Could it be possible?

Change my mind.

Moisture stung her eyes and one sole tear rolled down her cheek. Emotions welled up and a soft cautious beam of hope began to glow inside her. Was the indomitable man finally softening to her? Would he be willing to listen and really hear what she had to say?

Maybe one day soon. Sophia wouldn't press her luck tonight, but she would meet with him. They would go on their first date, and she would see where that would take them.

There was hope now, that her love would not be wasted.

Logan hadn't been to the cemetery since his father's funeral. But today he found himself standing over his parents' graves with a bouquet of roses in his hands. He stared at the headstones, wondering about his father and mother's relationship. To a boy who only saw what was right in front of him, Logan had thought his parents loved each other. He had thought that their family was as strong and as sturdy as the Ponderosa pines. He had thought his father was the fairest, most honest man in the world.

It was all a facade to conceal the truth. His father had lied and had conspired to destroy the family by abandoning his mother and bringing Louisa Montrose into the picture.

New anger rose up now as he gazed at their graves. The only crime his mother had committed in all of this was to love Randall Slade and expect his loyalty in return. After his mother found out about the affair, she'd protected her family by firing Louisa Montrose and banishing her and Sophia from the ranch. Ivy had forged on, raising her sons and loving a man who didn't love her in return. In Logan's mind, Ivy Slade was a hero—a woman who'd born great injury living in a house with a man who had betrayed and humiliated her.

"I'm sorry, Mom," he said, his voice nearly breaking. He bent on one knee to brush away dried blades of grass and fallen leaves from her headstone. And then he laid the dozen buttercup roses down—her favorite—keeping the flat of his hand on the headstone. This was his time with his mother. Every couple of months, he spent just a few minutes here where he could feel a connection to her.

It was the second time today Logan had offered up flowers. He'd sent Sophia flowers this morning, and she'd sent him a message that she would be ready tonight at eight o'clock for their first date.

Logan wondered if he was a hypocrite to lay tremendous blame on his father, when Logan himself had been lured in by a Montrose. Yet he understood a man's weakness when mind and body were involved. Sophia had gotten under his skin. She was like an addiction. He had to have her, but he'd taken his father's failures to heart. He'd learned a valuable lesson and he'd vowed to never let himself become vulnerable to Sophia.

He could make the distinction, between lust and love.

With that notion in mind, Logan pivoted on his heels and got into his truck. As he drove out of the cemetery, he turned on the radio. Brad Paisley's voice carried over the airwaves with lyrics that touted the joys of fishing. Logan sang along with him, his mood lighter and anticipation stirring in his gut. Tonight, he had a date with a beautiful woman.

Four hours later, Logan rapped on Sophia's bedroom door, hat in hand. He hadn't seen her since this morning. A classic oil-painting image of her had stayed in his head all day—Sophia standing nude, one hip elevated, the curve of her feminine body inviting and the look in her eyes enticing. It had taken every ounce of his willpower to walk away from her. But he couldn't lie to her. He couldn't tell her the things she wanted to hear, so he'd done what he had to do.

She opened the door and gave him a small smile. "Hi." One large gold hoop dangled from her ear. "Come in," she said, turning and walking toward her dressing mirror.

Logan followed behind her.

"Sorry, I'm running late," she said, putting on the other earring as she faced the mirror.

"No problem." Logan stood beside her. Watching Sophia put the finishing touches on her outfit wasn't a hardship.

"We had a last-minute emergency at the lodge. The sprinkler system went off right in the middle of our barbecue dinner. Everyone went scrambling and we—"

Logan cut her off with a brief kiss. "Let's not talk about work tonight," he said.

He took a step back as the delicious taste of her mouth got his juices flowing. He couldn't imagine concentrating on irritated guests or broken sprinkler systems with the way Sophia looked tonight. Her hair was up in some sort of pretty curly twist at the top of her head. Her short gold dress glimmered and draped in soft folds over her chest. It was cinched at her slender waist, accentuating her female curves and hugging her thighs. Jeweled sandals encased her feet.

"O-okay," she said, touching the back of her hair nervously. "No business tonight then."

"You look amazing, Sophia."

Her scent perfumed the air. It was the same tempting fragrance she'd worn last night when they'd been dueling between the sheets. It wasn't a smell he would soon forget.

"Thank you. I wasn't sure how to dress. Your note didn't say where we were going."

He rubbed the back of his neck. "Yeah, well…I wasn't sure you'd accept my invitation."

Her tawny eyes lifted to study his face. "You sent lovely flowers, but it was what you wrote that made me agree."

Logan winced inwardly. He shouldn't have written what he had. He wasn't sure he would ever follow through and change his mind. But this morning after the hot erotic night they'd shared, he'd been thinking with a brain located south of his belt buckle.

He'd made no promises to Sophia though. And he clung to that reasoning as he put his hand to the luscious curve of her back, leading her from the bedroom and out of the house.

"You're not working tomorrow," he said after he helped her slip into the passenger's side of his car.

"I don't have to go in until the afternoon. But, Logan," she said, with a warning in her voice.

"We're taking a drive and we'll be out late. That's all I meant, little Ms. Suspicious."

Sophia chuckled and the sweet sound filled his head.

"I want to show you something."

"Is it a secret?" she asked.

"Sorta."

Sophia's voice got higher. "Really?"

Logan nodded. He wasn't quite sure why he'd decided to bring Sophia to the spot he had in mind except that it was important that he impress her. "It's a special place."

"For all of your first dates?"

Sophia was fishing for clues, but he didn't mind answering her truthfully. "You're the first woman I'm taking there."

Sophia opened her mouth to say something, but then those full lips clamped down and she shot him a skeptical look.

He shrugged. "You don't have to believe me. But it's true."

"Does this place have a name?"

He gave her a nod. "The Hideaway."

Her brows gathered. "I've never heard of it."

"Exactly my point, darlin'. Now sit back and relax. It's an hour's drive from here."

Carved out of a mountainside, The Hideaway was a chateau overlooking a vast sea of sugar pine trees with bulky trunks and branches lifting skyward like regal green giants. Beyond the forest, the still waters of Lake Tahoe glistened in the distance under starry moonlight. Lights wrapped around garden posts twinkled near where Sophia stood on the terrace outside the restaurant. She leaned against a square column, looking out. Peace and contentment filled her.

Logan walked up and handed her a glass of sparkling water.

"Thank you," she said, gazing out. She took a sip of her drink. The cool lime-flavored liquid bubbled and popped on the way down her throat.

"I thought you might like it here." He held a glass in his hand. She was pretty sure it was scotch.

"You own The Hideaway, don't you?" she asked.

Logan had driven up a narrow mountain road to get here and when they'd arrived, Sophia had been surprised by what she'd found—a restaurant designed with a European rustic flare nestled in the woods. Porcelain tile work lay beneath her feet and textured walls surrounded her. The dining room had private seating areas with tufted embroidered sofas and love seats. Atop a travertine fireplace mantel half a dozen pillar candles burned, casting soft shadows on the walls.

"You catch on fast." His teasing smile was so genuine and rare that Sophia found herself staring at his mouth. He looked handsome in a three-piece Western suit with a brocade vest, but when he flashed his pearly whites her heart raced.

"The empty restaurant and the little tour you gave introducing me to the chef and his staff were dead giveaways."

He grinned. "I can't fool you. The food's pretty good. The place is quiet. And the view is…"

"Magnificent," she whispered in awe. Her gaze wandered over the trees to the shimmering silver lake as she took in the natural splendor.

"Yeah, it is." His tone made her turn away from the sugar pines to face him.

He stared at her a long moment, his eyes piercing her soul. He took a sip of his scotch and shook his head as if trying to clear out his thoughts.

"What is it?" she asked softly.

He drew a deep breath. "Nothing."

But it was something. He'd looked tormented for a second. The amused gleam in his eyes evaporated—he'd gone to some distant place—and regret marred his handsome expression.

"We can eat anytime you want," he said, transforming his expression to produce a charming smile. "The chef has prepared something special for us."

Sophia wouldn't question Logan further. She refused to let her mind go to a dark place of doubt and uncertainty. Maybe she'd only imagined the tortured look on his face. "I would love to try the chef's specialty."

Logan showed her to a table that was in the prettiest corner of the room. She was well aware that he had closed down the restaurant for a private meal with her. She couldn't say she wasn't impressed and flattered. "Do you go to such trouble for all your first dates?"

"I can honestly tell you, no, I don't."

His declaration made Sophia extremely happy. "More like a Kickin' Kitchen kind of thing then?"

"Don't disparage Kickin'. The food's great when you know your limits."

Sophia raised her brows but she let Logan get away with that jibe. She was glad to see his mood lighten. "So how long have you owned this place?"

"Six months."

"I think it's a wonderful chateau but I'm a little surprised."

"Because I'm a rancher and this isn't really in my wheelhouse?"

Sophia didn't want to pry but she was curious, so she gave him a slight nod.

"My friend owned the place, but he couldn't make it work. His managerial skills were not up to snuff. He was losing business, about to go into foreclosure." Logan shrugged as if buying a business was an everyday occurrence for him. "I don't like to see beautiful things fall to ruin, and in this case,

I could do something about it. I saved my friend's ass and bought it at a fair price."

Sophia glanced around the entire restaurant. It was cozy and warm and elegant. "Your friend is very lucky."

"It was business."

"Maybe," Sophia said. "Or maybe you're more softhearted than you think."

"Definitely...*not*."

Logan finished off the last ounce of his scotch. He could be a hard-ass at times, but Sophia knew there was a softer side to Logan Slade, whether or not he wanted to admit it. When his guard was down, Sophia figured him to be a pretty decent man. Then a thought struck. "Isn't Luke staying somewhere close by?"

Logan studied her for a few long moments. "He's on the other side of the lake, some twenty miles of winding road from here." In a clipped voice, he asked, "Why? You want to stop by for a visit?"

She heard masked resentment in his tone. Logan and Luke were at odds lately and it was best for her not to interfere. Though she missed Luke and hoped he was doing well, she didn't know how he would take the news about her being in love with Logan. She'd avoided calling him and felt like a heel about it, but she didn't know how to broach the subject about her and Logan. Everything was up in the air anyway. Sophia had no clue what the future held for them. What could she say to Luke?

I've moved into your house and slept with your brother.

"What I want is to be right here with you," she said honestly.

Logan seemed satisfied with her reply. He gave a quick nod. "My brother's doing okay."

"I'm happy to hear that."

The subject was dropped and dinner was served. It was the most exquisite melt-in-your-mouth meal Sophia had ever eaten—a dish with tender herb-infused sirloin strips and shi-take mushrooms along with delicately grilled then lightly fried vegetables. Summoning her bravado, she broached a question that had been on her mind. "What was your relationship like with your father after my mother and I left Sunset Ranch?"

Logan's lips tightened and he moved his empty plate away a little more forcefully than necessary. "Why do you want to know?"

Sophia toyed with her hair, curling a loose strand around her finger. "I always wondered what happened after we left."

Logan rubbed the underside of his chin, contemplating for a second, then gave a sigh before responding. "I hated him."

His admission wasn't a surprise. She'd come to understand a boy's disillusionment over a man he'd once idolized. She could sympathize with Logan now, and feel the pain he must have endured. Her situation hadn't been all that different in terms of the pain she'd felt over her father, although Sophia hadn't known him. She'd been too young, but his betrayal had affected her life regardless. He'd hurt her mother and had abandoned his family. Growing up fatherless, Sophia had lived with the hurt and hatred inside for many years. "I'm sorry."

"I'm thinking you really are," he said, but before their eyes could hold a connection, Logan looked away.

"Do you still hate him?" Sophia spoke in a hushed tone, hoping to keep this conversation going.

Logan winced. "What difference does it make now? He's gone."

"Forgiveness heals."

Logan began shaking his head. "I'm not there yet, Sophia. Let's not be spoiling our date with this kind of talk."

Sophia didn't mean to push him, but she was falling deeper and deeper in love with him. She wanted everything out in the open, so they could cut a clear path together without any obstacles getting in their way. He'd asked her to change his mind, but she couldn't do that unless he was willing to discuss painful memories. But it was obvious, tonight was not the night. "You're right. We'll talk of other things."

Logan rose from his seat and announced, "We'll have dessert out on the terrace, if that's all right with you."

Sophia stood. "Yes, I'd like that."

"Good. I'm in need of fresh air."

Logan put a hand to her waist just as she pivoted and their bodies brushed intimately. She stood inches from him, her face lifted to his. "I'm sorry, Logan. I didn't mean to upset you."

He moved even closer and something intense flared in his eyes. "The only thing upsetting me is not being able to touch you."

"You've touched me," she whispered.

His head angled down and he murmured softly, blowing warm breath over her ear. "Not the way I want. I'm on first-date best behavior."

Sophia sucked oxygen into her lungs. "You get an A for effort and a big, gold star."

His mouth hovered near hers and their breaths mingled. "I'd rather have a kiss."

Surprised, she smiled softly but Logan didn't wait for her permission. He took her in a leisurely kiss filled with enough delicious promise to break down all of her defenses, all of her firm resolutions.

Dessert was abandoned and they drove home quietly holding hands and sharing heated glances in the car.

When Logan escorted her into the house, there wasn't a doubt in her mind where she would sleep tonight. Whatever this was between them, whatever Logan thought of her and however she was supposed to change his mind, she couldn't stop the compelling magnetism that linked her to him. She couldn't deny what seemed like her destiny.

She placed her faith in him, depending on his sense of fairness and decency. Judging by their personal history it was a giant leap for her to make.

Logan wouldn't betray her trust, would he?

Nine

Sophia had never slept with a man on a first date, and with wry amusement she decided that waking up in Logan's bed this morning after an incredible bout of lovemaking was worth the distinction. Making love in the tack room the other night didn't count. At least in her sleep-groggy mind it didn't. She rationalized that that had been an impulse born of desire and lust with no promise of the future. She'd been seduced by something far greater than her own willpower. But ever since Logan had sent her flowers and written a note claiming he was going to try, asking her out on a genuine, pull-out-all-stops kind of date, Sophia had come to conclusions that meant lowering her guard and taking a risk.

The evening had been magical for her. And when Logan actually gave her a chaste good-night kiss, attempting to keep his promise of best first-date behavior, Sophia had put a halt to the charade. She'd taken Logan's hand and together they walked into his bedroom with no words spoken.

Now, Sophia lay sprawled out on his bed, a soft cotton sheet covering her naked body and a smile on her lips.

Logan walked into the room and whipped off her covers. "Wake up, sleepyhead."

"Mmm," she said, grabbing for the covers. "I'm being lazy before I have to go into work."

"What? And leave all this?" Logan shook his head. "You're not going into work today, honey," he announced. "I have it all arranged."

"I wish you weren't kidding."

"I'm not." He winked and spoke with smug satisfaction. "Your meetings are postponed and Lois Benson will cover for you today. She's in line for assistant manager and she's eager to prove herself. Besides, I have the day planned for us."

Sophia was beside herself with joy. She didn't have anything pressing on her schedule today and the idea of spending the entire day with Logan was beyond appealing. "Does it involve more sleeping in this big comfy bed?"

Logan bent to land a solid kiss on her mouth. "It does involve this bed, sweetheart, I will damn well guarantee you that."

Sophia chuckled and laid back on the mattress. But her rest was short-lived before Logan whisked her up into his arms. "First I think you need to try out my shower."

"Are you joining me?" she asked, intrigued with the notion, kicking her legs playfully as he carried her toward the bathroom.

"Sure am. I have to show you what buttons and knobs to turn on."

Sophia giggled and just minutes later they were soapy and steamy and covered with moisture. Logan loved her with his mouth until she was adequately tortured and fully spent. Sophia coaxed a similar response from him when she put her lips around the silky skin sheathing his manhood. The intense sound of three showerheads raining down couldn't drown out

Logan's groans of completion. He held her tight in his arms as the water continued to cleanse them.

"You're an amazing man," Sophia said, her heart bursting. She'd almost told him how much she loved him then but at the last moment she held back, too unsure of his reaction.

"We are good together, Sophia," he murmured, sprinkling kisses over her throat, her chin and her lips. She closed her eyes and held on for dear life, her emotions threatening to overwhelm her.

The rest of the day was spent riding mares along a stream that ran through the backwoods of Slade property, stopping for a picnic lunch near the trickling waters and making lazy, crazy love in the middle of nowhere on a blanket by the stream's bank. It was the perfect day and later that evening when they'd returned to Sunset Ranch, they got comfortable in Logan's bed and watched old classic Westerns. Sophia fell asleep in Logan's arms never feeling more content.

The next week was blissful heaven. Sophia shared her mornings and nights with Logan Slade. She'd wake to kisses drizzled on her cheek from a man who was seriously dangerous to her equilibrium. They'd shower and dress, and then eat a light breakfast together before going their separate ways. Sophia poured her concentration into Sunset Lodge, working as hard as she could to prove to herself and Logan that she was capable and deserved the inheritance Randall Slade had bestowed upon her. She beamed inside and that spark kept a smile on her face through every task, every duty she took on.

Logan seemed happy, too, for the most part. But every once in a while she'd catch him in a moment when his expression would falter, as if something cold and foreboding had wrestled itself into his mind. When that happened, dreadful shivers crept up her spine.

If there was any buzz about her relationship with Logan at the ranch or Sunset Lodge, it hadn't reached Sophia's ears.

There wasn't much she could do about it if there was. She wasn't going to let gossip stand in the way of what she wanted.

She never had.

On Thursday afternoon, Sophia sat at her office desk and typed in a text message to Luke. How is my friend doing today?

A couple of days ago, Sophia had decided the best way to avoid a conversation she didn't want to have with Logan's brother was to text him. She could use a minimum of words to ask how he was doing and those brand-new audio texting applications allowed him to answer. For a man with a broken arm and healing ribs, voice-activated texting couldn't be beat.

She received an immediate message back. I'm healing. Feeling better every day. Miss you and the ranch.

I miss you, too, but all is well here. She punched in three smiley faces and decided that was over the top. She erased two of them, and then hit Send. Conversation over.

She was a coward. She admitted it. Logan wouldn't tell Luke what was going on between them. It landed on Sophia's shoulders, but it was an awkward situation to say the least. So she'd avoided the subject altogether. She was concerned for Luke, but yet her lack of courage kept her from having a real conversation with him.

The sound of Blackie's sharp barks took her out of her deep thoughts. She got up from her desk and walked out of her office in search of the dog. She exited through the lobby doors and walked along the path toward the side of the lodge. She chuckled when she spotted Blackie jumping off the ground, all four legs in midair at once as Edward teased him with a rib bone. The dog nearly toppled the boy over trying to get to the bone.

Edward cackled with laughter and Sophia's mood lightened. She walked up to them, and both boy and dog stopped playing.

"Hello, Edward. I see you have something Blackie wants."

Edward looked at her shyly. She hadn't seen the boy around for a while. "Y-yes, ma'am."

"And hello to you, too, Blackie."

The dog forgot about the bone, and with tail wagging, came over to her. She bent down to stroke his coat and Blackie's head tilted to one side, his tongue hanging out in a true doggie smile. "Are you behaving yourself?"

His tail wagged faster.

"He is. He h-hasn't come into N-Nana's kitchen a-again ever." Edward, always ready to come to Blackie's defense, stuck the bone into his back pocket, out of sight of the dog for now.

"That's good." Sophia gave Blackie a last pat and, rising, turned her attention to the boy. "How have you been, Edward?"

He looked at her and then glanced down. "F-fine."

"I haven't seen you too much lately."

"I d-don't have any h-homework today."

"Oh, that's explains it, you've been busy studying. I used to love those days best when the teacher gave us a day off. Do you still like to hike, Edward?"

He nodded. "I go with Mr. S-Slade some-t-times."

"I would love to hike with you, too, when school is out. Would that be all right?"

His face turned crimson and a small smile emerged. He was a sweet boy. Sophia tried her best to put him at ease and let him know she was his friend. He darted a glance toward the cottage, his eyes wide with curiosity and an unspoken question on his lips. He had to be curious why she wasn't living there anymore. It wasn't an easy thing to explain to a ten-year-old boy. "We'll make plans for that hike as soon as summer starts, okay?"

"Okay."

"Well, you and Blackie have a nice day. I just wanted to say hello to both of you. I'll see you again soon."

The rib bone reappeared and Edward gave it a toss. Sophia put her hand over her brows, shadowing her eyes from the blazing sunlight as she watched Blackie digging in, outrunning Edward in a race for his treat.

Seeing the boy was a nice diversion, a break in the long day she'd needed. She had two hours left of work before she would see Logan again and she would count the minutes.

As she made her way along the flowery path to the lodge's entrance she stopped short when a black stretch limousine caught her eye. It pulled to stop under the portico and a chauffeur dressed in a tan uniform got out.

A gasp escaped her as memories rushed through her mind. She recognized that limo with the famous script *G* emblazoned on the side doors. The driver opened the passenger door and two men exited. One was the deadly handsome cowboy she loved and the other was her older, distinguished, wealthy ex-husband, Gordon Gregory. He was medium height, blue-eyed and not bad-looking for an older man, wrinkles and all. He dressed impeccably and had a full head of silver hair.

Seeing the two men together made her heart pound. One man might be her future—the other was her past. She took a big swallow and stood there immobilized, looking to Logan first. His expression was unreadable. Gordon, on the other hand, smiled.

Darn, this was the last thing she needed. She and Logan were working things out and becoming closer. How would he react seeing her ex-husband and being reminded of the worst thing he'd thought about her?

"Hello, my beautiful Sophia." Gordon's possessive tone made her uneasy.

Logan slid him a disapproving look.

"Hello, Gordon. What are you doing here?"

"He came to buy a stallion," Logan said through tight lips. "We've just had a good talk."

Sophia's face flamed and she cringed inside. Had they

been talking about her? When she'd married Gordon it had been out of desperate need. He'd been wonderful and kind in the beginning and so grateful about his granddaughter that she'd thought she was doing the right thing for her mother when she'd married him. She'd fooled herself into thinking she could come to love him in time. He'd promised her a marriage with no strings attached. Maybe she'd been a little naive to actually believe that, but at the time, Sophia hadn't been looking to the future. She'd been focused on the present and the best way to help her mother. Shortly after her mother passed away, Gordon's expectations had changed and so had his attitude. He'd come on strong in the guise of helping her grieve for Louisa. And one night he'd blurted that his debt to her had been paid in full. They were on even ground now and it was time for Sophia to start acting like a wife to him. He'd boxed her into a corner and there was only one way out that she could see. She'd ended the marriage.

"I couldn't stop by Sunset Ranch and not come by for a visit," he went on. "Logan here was kind enough to show me to the lodge. I'd like a private word with you, my dear. Now would be a good time."

She felt Logan's eyes on her as he spoke firmly to Gordon. "*Only* if it's a good time for Sophia. Is it?"

The older man's brows flew up and he chuckled. "I see. She's got you under her spell already. I can't really blame you. She's quite a woman. You should have seen her on that cho- rus line. She was a standout, destined to become a headliner."

Sophia's stomach began to ache. Gordon's appearance here threatened to undermine the reputation she'd tried to live down with Logan. "I have a few minutes, Gordon."

"Fine, fine." When Gordon reached for Sophia's arm, Logan stepped between them and faced her, turning his back on the older man. "Are you sure you have time for this guy?" he asked her. "I could care less about the sale of the stallion."

Sophia wanted to kiss him for intervening, for making

sure Gordon didn't lay a hand on her. Especially since, for all Logan knew, Sophia had been intimate with the older man. "I'm sure."

Logan nodded, and for a second she noted a hint of accusation in his eyes. "I'll see you later."

"I'll be there," she whispered softly before turning to Gordon. "We can talk in my office."

She led the way, keeping one step ahead of him. Once she climbed the steps to the entrance, she opened the door and turned. Logan stood grounded to the spot, his gaze keen and sharp, missing nothing.

There's nothing to see, Logan. No great conspiracy. No gold-digging.

Sophia walked with her chin high and her mind reeling. Why on earth was Gordon here? She entered her office and settled behind her desk, pointing to a chair. "Please have a seat."

The elderly man lowered himself with regal authority. "You've moved on, Sophia. I take it you've snagged that rich cowboy and convinced him to let you run this place."

"Actually, you and I both know I inherited half ownership of Sunset Lodge. I'm sure you've done your homework, Gordon. And I doubt a man like Logan Slade would allow anyone to *snag* him," she added.

"Ah, but if a woman could do it, it would be you," he said.

That just showed how little Gordon really knew about the situation. Logan had tried to bribe her to get her to leave the ranch just weeks ago.

"How is Amanda?"

He seemed pleased that she'd asked. "My granddaughter is doing very well. She lost a year of high school during that crazy time, but she's on the right road now. She'll be starting college in the fall."

Sophia's heart warmed. Amanda had been a mixed-up kid who'd needed guidance in her life and some professional counseling. Sophia was glad to have helped her see that her life was worth salvaging. "I'm glad to hear it. Please give her my best."

"I will."

"What can I help you with?" She tilted her head, still curious why he'd shown up here. She knew darn well buying a horse wasn't the only reason. That had been the excuse.

He smiled again, his eyes crinkling heavily at the corners. "I came to buy a stallion and I have, but I'm also here to honor a promise I made to Louisa."

At the mention of her mother's name, Sophia's shoulders slumped and she was struck with immediate sadness. All of the brassiness she'd summoned to deal with Gordon disappeared. "Wh-what promise?"

"To make sure you were all right. To make sure you were safe. You see, your mother may have pretended not to know how sick she was, but she knew. We would have candid talks about it. Louisa and I had actually become very close in the end. She never wanted you to worry. She knew you had enough to deal with. You marrying me gave your mother peace of mind."

She'd hoped so. With her whole heart, she had truly hoped so. Sophia closed her eyes, momentarily absorbing the truth of his words. Her mother always pretended to feel better than she actually felt to ease Sophia's mind. She'd been a trouper about her treatments and always tried to put a smile on her face even when her health had begun to decline. Sophia wished she could be as strong and capable and caring a woman as her mother had been.

"I think she would've liked you to stay married to me," Gordon said.

"I might have, if you hadn't pressured me."

"I was very patient with you, Sophia. I was good to you."

"Yes, I can't deny that. You were very good to my mother and me."

"So can you blame me for wanting a real wife? Your mother was gone, God rest her soul, and you were safe, away from a stalker's threats. I figured—"

"I'd owe you?"

"No, Sophia. I had hoped you'd have real affection for me."

"I appreciate everything you did for me, but contrary to what some might believe, I can't be bought. You put pressure on me shortly after my mother died and made me very uncomfortable. Gordon, you're not a man who takes no lightly. You pressed me until I had no choice but to walk away."

Gordon actually looked contrite. "I'm sorry. It was a mistake on my part to pressure you. I'm a bit spoiled. I usually get what I want and, beautiful Sophia, you were my wife."

Sophia had walked away without a dime of Gordon's great wealth. She'd insisted on a prenup that said exactly that. She'd never wanted his money. She'd never wanted to be beholden to Gordon. "I know," she whispered, "but I couldn't give you what you wanted."

Gordon put his head down. He steepled his fingers and spoke quietly. "You may think me a silly old man for saying so, but I fell in love with you, Sophia."

Sophia was touched and she believed him, but Gordon Gregory fell in love a lot. He'd been married and divorced five times in his seventy-one years. "And you deserve a woman in your life who will give you love back."

"I see that now." A shrug rolled off his shoulder. "Well... I've done my part, Sophia. I've checked on you for Louisa's sake. I see you've made a life for yourself here. Are you happy?"

Sophia didn't have to think twice. "Yes."

He nodded and gave her a thoughtful look. "Then I'd venture to guess Logan Slade is a very lucky man."

After Sophia bid farewell to Gordon, she sat in her office staring at the paperwork on her desk. The numbers on the account sheets made no sense. She wouldn't even try to turn on her computer. She couldn't concentrate. She couldn't seem to think of much else but Gordon Gregory's appearance here today. She'd never expected him to seek her out. That part of her life, a trying, difficult part of her life, was over. Seeing Logan drive up in the limo with Gordon had really rattled her.

While she'd silently grieved for her mother all these months, speaking with Gordon today and hashing over their lives had brought fresh pain to her heart. From her grave, her mother was still trying to look out for her—still trying to protect her. It served to make Sophia miss her mother even more.

She'd married a man for what he could give her, yes. But it wasn't a selfish money-grubbing move. It had been for her mother's sake. Gordon had provided safe haven in his mansion for both the Montrose women and hopefully now that she'd grown closer to Logan, he would believe her.

With that resolved in her mind, Sophia managed to struggle through her work. Apprehension gripped her stomach tight. Logan had been a wonderful lover and they'd shared so much with each other, but the one thing that Sophia needed from him now was his willingness to see her in a different light. It mattered now. So much. She wanted his trust. She wanted him to believe in her.

The brim on his hat cocked low, Hunter Halliday gave a light rap at her opened office door. "It's that time," he said, stepping one foot into the office.

For the past week, Hunter had come in the late afternoon to alert her it was time to feed the horses. Aside from her time spent with Logan, hand-feeding the horses with Hunter was the best part of her day. "Thank goodness. I am so ready to call it a day."

Hunter waited for her to straighten her desk and lock up the office. They walked out the side door that led toward the lodge stables, making pleasant small talk. Several of the lodge guests were about, the scent of horse dung and straw giving them the full ranch-type experience. She waved to them and walked farther down to where Hunter kept a jumbo-sized bag of carrots.

At the corral, five horses trotted over and nudged each other out of the way trying to get their fair share of food. Sophia let each horse take a carrot out of her palm and then patted their foreheads, one right after the other. Hunter took a few carrots over to an elderly couple who stood watching from several feet away. He gave them each a turn feeding the horses.

Sophia walked over to them. "They love getting extra treats."

The woman smiled. "Well, then we'll have to come by tomorrow at this time, too."

Hunter agreed and started up a conversation with the two of them while Sophia bid them farewell. Her mood lighter, she felt a little better about talking to Logan tonight.

"Ms. Montrose?" Hunter called as she approached her car. "You heading over to the main house?"

"Yes, I am."

"Will you say hello to Luke for me?"

Confused, Sophia gave Hunter a shake of the head. *"Luke?"*

"Yes, ma'am. I saw him going into the house an hour ago. Luke's back."

Ten

A knot formed in Sophia's stomach as she parked her Camry by the ranch house garage. She sat in the car a minute, still unsure what to do about Luke. If Logan was home, maybe he'd already had a conversation with him. Or maybe he'd left that privilege for her. Sophia had wanted a little more time with Logan. And after her visit from Gordon today, she'd hoped she could be honest and up-front about things he didn't want to talk about. She'd hoped she could make headway with him. It would require faith and trust on both their parts.

Sadly, she still didn't have a clear definition of her relationship with Logan. And she still didn't know what she would say to Luke. She got out of the car and made her way toward the house, wondering if she could find the right words. Deep in thought, she climbed the steps and entered the house, closing the door behind her.

Instantly, two booming male voices resounding from the long hallway stopped her cold. She couldn't make out the words, but she certainly knew harsh tones when she heard them. And it was clear that Logan and Luke were butting heads again. When she heard her name mentioned, Sophia moved down the hallway, compelled by a force stronger than good etiquette allowed to secretly listen to the two men she cared most about. She leaned against the outside wall of Logan's office, out of sight.

"You're telling me that Sophia has moved into the house?" Luke's voice was full of his displeasure.

Logan's impatient words rang out. "I told you about the threats at the cottage."

"So she's here for her own safety?"

"There's more. We're not going to tiptoe around now that you're home."

"Meaning what?"

Logan's voice carried a distinct certainty. "Meaning she's with me now."

There was a long pause, and Sophia squeezed her eyes shut. She didn't know what to expect from this conversation. Logan hadn't been subtle or taken the time to ease Luke into the idea.

"You son of a bitch." Disbelief reverberated off the walls. "You're sleeping with her."

"That's right, Luke. It's a mutual arrangement."

Again there was a long pause as Luke absorbed that for a minute. Sophia didn't know if she should make her presence known, but his next words made her rethink revealing herself until she'd heard Logan's answer.

"So then you've forgiven her of all crimes? You don't think she's out for our money?"

"I didn't say that."

"You're not cutting her any slack, are you?" Luke asked angrily.

"I'm watching our backs, Luke."

"You're going to hurt her and if you do, I'll—"

"I'm making damn well sure you don't hook up with her.

You'd be foolish enough to fall in love with her. At least with me, I know that'll never happen. I'm protecting our interests."

"You're a bastard, Logan." Luke's words were sharp, cutting. "Sophia deserves better than that."

Logan lashed back, "Yeah, what do you know? You didn't wake up one night and wander into the barn as a kid to find our father, the esteemed Randall Slade, sprawled over her mother in the tack room. The two of them were going at it—"

Sophia gasped. Stunned, she moved on shaky legs into the office doorway. The Slade men both looked up at the same time, shocked to see her standing there in full view.

She felt the blood drain from her face. Her body went limp as she faced Logan. She'd overheard everything. Logan had never cared for her. He'd never fall in love with her. She took a swallow, having to look deep into his eyes and hear him repeat the one thing that brought it all together. The one thing that proved his wicked deception.

"The t-tack room, Logan?"

Logan's hard eyes softened. "Sophia."

Luke let out a curse. "Don't listen to him, Sophia. He's an—"

"Answer me, Logan," she demanded, raising her voice. Luke wouldn't understand why this was so devastating to her. "You saw our parents together in the *tack* room?"

Logan blinked and began shaking his head. "You weren't meant to hear this conversation."

Sophia couldn't breathe. Her chest pounded and her stomach twisted in agony. She'd never felt so completely betrayed. This was all a game to Logan—and a way to keep her away from Luke. He must have had a good long laugh over it when he seduced her in the very place he'd found his father making love to her mother. She was at a loss so profound a cold wave wrapped around her body and threatened to freeze her out. It was as if the light beaming inside her died. She was numb and brokenhearted, but forces from deep within would not allow her to walk out of here until Logan heard the truth.

"First of all, Luke is right. You're a bastard."

Logan flinched, which gave her a measure of satisfaction. The man wasn't made entirely of stone. If her words cut him, they were only a tiny tear, unlike the way she'd been ripped apart.

"You've never wanted to hear the truth about your parents. I've wanted to tell you but I thought I should wait until I had your trust. But I see now I'll never have that. Luke, you should know this, too. When your mother and father married it was more an arrangement to bring two powerful ranching families together. There was never great passion between them. Randall married because she'd gotten pregnant with you. He didn't love her the way she wanted to be loved though. The way every woman deserves to be loved. But your mother and father did merge the ranches and did build a family together."

Sophia put her head down. She couldn't bear to see the look of pain in Logan's expression. After a few seconds, she forged on. He needed to hear this. Even if he didn't believe her, she owed this to her mother and to herself. She faced Logan again, looking him straight in the eyes, holding back her tears. "When we came to live at the ranch, there was nothing between my mother and your father but mutual respect. Over the years, they grew closer and fought the attraction with everything they had but eventually they fell deeply in love. My mother was tormented. I would hear her crying during the night. Often she'd speak of leaving the ranch, of finding another job somewhere else. But I loved living here. I loved it so much and I couldn't understand at the time why my mother wanted to leave. I pleaded with her to stay on. I couldn't bear the thought of not living at the cottage or on Sunset Ranch. So we stayed."

Early memories of her mother's sadness were fresh in her mind. Sophia remembered her mother crying and the defeat in her voice in those brief moments when she'd let her guard down. It had been a painful time for her. "Your father was set to divorce Ivy. It wasn't an easy decision for him but he'd been determined. My mother stopped him. She wouldn't allow Randall to break up his family for her. Everyone thought that Ivy found out about their affair and fired my mother. But the truth was that my mother went to Ivy to apologize. She offered to move away so that she and Randall could patch up their relationship and keep the family together. Mama always told me she'd done the right thing. She couldn't have lived with herself if she'd broken up your family. She never took a penny of Randall's money and she made him promise to never follow her. To my knowledge he never did."

"But he did provide for you in his will," Luke pointed out.

The room got quiet. Logan's face masked his emotions.

"My mother loved Randall Slade with her whole heart and she gave him up. It was the hardest thing she ever had to do." Sophia choked up then and tears spilled from her eyes when she looked at Logan one last time. "Mama…always said…it was a waste of love."

His dark eyes flickered and he moved toward her. But Sophia backed away, putting out a hand warning him not to come closer. "I'm moving back into the cottage. I want to be left alone. I hope both of you will respect my wishes."

"Sophia, me?" Luke asked.

Warmth filled her heart for the man who was her friend. It was a blessing to see Luke looking so fit, regardless of the cast on his arm. She could barely breathe, barely talk. Her words were soft, a quiet plea for Luke's understanding. "I'm sorry, but I need to be alone right now."

She turned then, and walked out the door. She'd never had hope torn from her body this way before. She'd never had such devastating disillusionment.

She missed her mother more now than ever before.

And she knew that she would miss loving Logan Slade almost as much.

Logan lowered down into his chair and squeezed his eyes shut. But the image of Sophia appeared in his head anyway. Her fiery spirit gone, she'd looked broken and beat down. Accusation and betrayal had marred her beautiful face.

The tack room, Logan?

Logan winced. It hadn't been planned. He hadn't set out to seduce her that night. It had been an ironic twist, a coincidence that Logan hadn't thought about until after the deed was done. When he realized he made love to her there, he hadn't put much significance in it. Until now. Until the angry words had slipped from his mouth during his argument with his brother and Sophia had overheard. He'd said brutal, harsh things about keeping Luke away from her, about how he would never fall in love with her. She'd heard it all.

Luke walked over to him, his voice menacing. "Stand up, so I can knock you on your ass."

Logan didn't bother to look at him. "With your left hand?"

"Jerk."

Logan's love/hate relationship with his brother was getting on his nerves. He wanted to be left alone with his miserable thoughts. "Get outta here, Luke."

"Sophia shouldn't be alone at the cottage."

"I know that," he snapped.

"I'll go over there tonight. She'll let me in. She *likes* me."

Logan stood now, and got directly in his brother's face. He felt the veins in his neck popping. "Don't go near her. If anyone's gonna protect her, it'll be me. You understand that?"

Luke opened his big mouth, but nothing came out. They stared at each other, practically nose to nose, and then Luke's eyes widened and he burst out laughing. Logan balled his fists.

"This is rich," Luke said when his laughter died down.
"You love her. You have fallen head over heels in love with
Sophia, and now she can't stand you. She'd rather risk a
stalker's threats than be under the same roof as you."

"You're delusional, bro."

"All this time you've been convincing yourself that Sophia is just like her mother. And it would serve you right to
find that she *was* exactly like Louisa—a goodhearted, kind
woman who deserved a break in life. A woman who made our
father happy for a short time. Hell, Logan. I knew Mom and
Dad weren't happy for years. They were partners in business
and they had kids to raise so they stuck it out. Their marriage
wasn't what you thought it was."

"You know this because you're the sensitive one and all."

"I didn't see Dad as a god. He was mortal and had human
flaws, just like the rest of us. I don't say what he did was right
and I know Dad did love Mom in his own way. They raised
us and managed to keep the family together. But maybe our
folks shouldn't have stayed together. Maybe they'd have both
been happier apart. Maybe you got it all wrong, Logan. Ever
think of that?"

Logan's nostrils flared. "I don't have it wrong."

"Okay, then fine. Let Sophia walk out of your life."

"She just did and I didn't go after her, did I?"

A look of disgust spread over Luke's face. "Your loss."

Logan watched his pain-the-ass brother turn around and
walk out of his office with slower than usual steps. The trip
home had taxed his strength but at least he did look stronger
than when he'd left. And the accident sure hadn't changed
his stubborn nature.

Once Logan was alone in his office, he made a call to add
extra security to the premises. He would drive by the cottage
tonight as well to check up on the place.

No one on Slade property would be in danger. He'd see to that.

Sophia included.

"I need your signatures here, here and here," Logan said, leaning over her desk pointing to three lines on a contract necessary for a revamping of the stables. The winters were harsh and the old barns needed new heating.

Logan had made it his business to stop by her office every day for the past five days for some reason or another. Every time he'd walked in she'd turned away, unwilling to meet him eye to eye. She knew he was checking up on her. She'd seen his car by the cottage on several occasions, but she also knew that Logan wasn't so much concerned about her welfare as he was about protecting his ranch from an intruder. He couldn't fool her any longer with a look or a smile. She knew his black heart now and even though the pain was still there, hovering like stormy gray clouds, Sophia was coping.

"Leave them and I'll read them over later." She used her very best business voice.

"I've had our attorney look them over. They are good to go."

Sophia nodded and signed on the dotted lines, shoving the papers back across the desk. She quickly withdrew her hands so their fingers wouldn't brush. She stepped back so she didn't have to breathe in his subtle earthy aftershave and be reminded of the nights they'd spent together.

"You're still not talking to me?" he asked.

"I talk to you every day." She was cool and dismissive on the outside, but inside her blood boiled. She prayed it would get easier seeing Logan each day. That he would leave her alone and let her go on with her life. Even when she was aloof with him, she sensed his eyes constantly on her, watching her movements.

Hands on hips, he stood over her desk and let out a frustrated sigh. "I never made false promises to you."

"Yes, you're right," she said. "You didn't." She wasn't going to go there. She wouldn't argue. She wouldn't defend. Her indifference was her only protection. "Now, is there anything else?"

"We can't go on working like this."

Sophia shut down her computer screen, still unwilling to look at him. "We won't have to. Luke's well enough to take over the lodge duties again. You're free as of today."

She heard Blackie's high-pitched barks from outside. Edward was probably on the grounds playing fetch with the dog. It was late afternoon and her work was finished for the day. She straightened the papers on her desk and rose. This time she cast a look at Logan. It was hard not to notice the way his clothes fit his body so perfectly, the stretch of soft cotton over his broad chest and jeans hugging his hips. There was a sexy five-o'clock shadow on his face and a tick went to town on his jaw. All of it made her heart do crazy things. It was dangerous to look at Logan. Dangerous to be so near.

"I have to go," she said quietly.

He spoke through tight lips. "Talk to me, Sophia."

"I can't. I have a…an appointment."

Logan's brows dented his forehead. "With who?"

She lifted her chin and kept her voice steady. "I'm having dinner with your brother."

Logan's face pinched tight. "Luke? Why in hell does it always come back to Luke?"

Sophia closed her eyes briefly, hoping to tamp down her emotions. Five minutes alone with Logan Slade was five minutes of torture. Heaven help her, she still loved him. "Because he's something to me that you never were, Logan. He's my friend. And right now I really need a friend."

As Sophia brushed by him, her nostrils drank in his scent. Leather and musk would be forever imprinted on her brain.

She had almost escaped the room when Logan spoke up. "What if I told you I'm green with jealousy over your friendship with my brother."

Sophia didn't move a muscle. She stood half in, half out of her office, her throat constricting. His admission had stunned her.

As a child, Logan had been the outsider, but purely of his own making. She and Luke would have welcomed him into their little friendship ring with open arms. But he'd never seen it that way. Logan had had a chip on his shoulder when it came to her. She'd always suspected Logan had thought she'd usurped his brother's attention.

She kept her back to him and spoke softly. "And what if I told you you could've been a part of our friendship? Luke adored his older brother and I would've accepted you as a friend."

She scurried out the door, fearing her own gentle heart. She couldn't bear to see Logan's expression now. A part of her hated him and a part of her felt sorry for the boy who'd been disillusioned so long ago.

Dinner at Dusty's Steakhouse was delicious and *safe,* Luke and Sophia having decided to leave the fire-alarm chili at Kickin' for another night. Her friend had been true to form, charming and fun-loving, and they'd had a few laughs. It was good to see Luke's health improve each day. But Sophia had been distracted all evening, struggling to keep her mind from jumping back to her conversation with Logan.

"What's wrong, Soph? Still can't get my brother out of your system?" Luke put his good arm around her shoulder in the friendly way he had as they walked up the cottage path.

"It's not that…exactly."

"Then what is it?"

She shrugged. She didn't want to ruin the peace of the night by talking about her problems with Logan. "Nothing. Sorry if I haven't been good company tonight."

"Don't be putting words in my mouth, Sophia. The company's fine. You've got something on your mind and I'd like to hear it."

Sophia stopped when she reached the entrance to the cottage. She turned to look into Luke's sky-blue eyes, wondering if she should be discussing Logan with his younger brother. The two men hardly got along, but she knew they loved each other. She didn't want to add fuel to the fire.

"Okay, if you're not going to tell me, let me guess. Logan said some other bonehead thing to you that's got you upset."

Sophia sighed and shook her head. "Not really...this is different."

"I'm surprised you're talking to him at all."

"You know I have to. Sunset Lodge is important to me. I can't let my personal life get in the way of my work."

His eyes lit with mischief. "Honey, I'm amazed you haven't slugged him yet, or kicked him in the—"

"Seriously, Luke," she said cutting him off. She'd never admit that the thought had crossed her mind to do both of those things to Logan in crazy fleeting moments of despair.

"Seriously, Sophia." Luke's voice grew softer, a plea from one friend to another. "You gonna tell me what my brother said to you?"

She looked away for a moment, nibbled on her lower lip and then finally answered Luke. "Logan admitted he was jealous of us when we were kids. I wasn't going to bring it up but—"

Disbelief and surprise crossed Luke's expression as his voice rose in pitch. "He thought you and I were—"

"No, no. Not in that way. He was jealous of our friendship. Did you know that?"

Luke's blond brows furrowed and he shook his head. "No, I never thought he gave a damn. Son of a gun. I thought we were too immature for him. He was always going on and on about how stupid we were, playing games, whispering secrets to each other. Doing things good friends do."

"Maybe he wanted to join us."

"Nah…I don't think so." Then Luke thought about it a moment. "But maybe."

Sophia nodded. "Yeah, maybe."

"If it was true, I'm kinda shocked he'd admit it to you now. It's not like Logan to confess something like that. Maybe the hard-hearted guy is finally softening up a bit. Even King Kong had a soft spot for a beautiful woman."

Sophia smiled at the reference comparing Logan to a giant ape.

"At least I made you smile."

She was grateful for Luke's company, but the stresses of the past week had taken their toll on her stamina. She tried to cover up a yawn and failed.

"You're beat," Luke said, stating the obvious.

She was. "Dinner was delicious."

"And this time you didn't wind up with a bellyache afterward."

"True."

She opened the front door and Luke stepped in behind her. She sent him an eye-roll and he just shrugged. "I'm outta here as soon as I find out where you hide the good stuff."

They'd had this disagreement in the restaurant, but in the end, Sophia agreed to let Luke inspect the cottage before he went home.

He moved down the hallway. The sound of doors opening and closing made her shake her head. There hadn't been any suspicious behavior or any more notes in days, thank goodness. Sophia was ready to put it all behind her. When Luke walked back into her parlor, he had a smile on his face. "Apparently you really don't drink. Couldn't even find a can of near beer."

"Thank you for checking. Now, let me get some sleep. I

have a big day of meetings tomorrow and they start first thing in the morning." Sophia rose on tiptoe. She touched her lips to his cheek in a chaste kiss. "Thanks for dinner."

Luke walked out the door and waited until he heard the click of the lock before bidding her farewell from her doorstep. "Sleep tight, Sophia."

"Good night, Luke."

It's hard not to love Sophia.

Gordon Gregory's parting shot had stuck in Logan's mind days after he'd sold Storm to the old geezer. Logan's response to the man's declaration had been an unintelligible grunt. He wasn't going to discuss Sophia with him. He'd believed that Gregory had come to the ranch to stir up trouble, and when he'd left that day Logan had done an internet search regarding his marriage to Sophia. He found that at one point, *Revealed* magazine had splashed Sophia's name across the front cover with a picture of her in full titillating Fantasy Follies costume. Logan had ground his teeth seeing her decked out in sequins barely covering her body with the old codger groping her waist.

Now as he stared at that cover shot on his office computer, he saw something he hadn't noticed before. When he'd looked at the picture, his focus had been on her body, shrink-wrapped into a showgirl's costume. Hell, any man would go there. She was perfect in all ways that mattered to men and it was natural to look at her full breasts, small waist and slender, smooth legs. But what he hadn't noticed before was the look in her eyes.

He studied those amber eyes now. They gave her away. There wasn't joy or contentment or even satisfaction on nabbing a rich man in those tawny depths. The photo revealed something entirely different. And for the first time since Sophia had come to Sunset Ranch, a shiver of cold dread worked its way down Logan's spine.

Logan had once made Sophia's eyes beam with joy. He'd made her eyes glow with contentment. He'd seen a look of sheer satisfaction spread across her beautiful face.

Marrying Gregory hadn't done any of those things for her.

Instead, the look in her eyes spoke of desperation and regret.

The phone rang, interrupting his thoughts. He picked it up and growled, "What?"

"Mr. Slade? It's Peggy Coswell from Human Resources at the lodge. I was wondering if…well, if you knew where Ms. Montrose is? She's late for our eight-o'clock meeting."

Logan glanced at the computer clock at the corner of his screen. "That was forty-five minutes ago."

"Yes, sir. She hasn't come into her office today."

Logan's heart beat faster. "Where else have you checked?"

"No one has seen her on the hotel grounds this morning. She's not answering her phone."

Fear gripped Logan's gut and twisted it like a pretzel. His mind turned to Luke. He'd had dinner with her last night. If he'd spent the night with Sophia… Logan's mind wouldn't go there. She wouldn't do that. Sophia just wouldn't sleep with his brother. And in that instant he knew two things. Sophia wasn't the kind of woman he'd made her out to be. She wasn't a gold-digging opportunist bent on getting rich any way she could. She wasn't out to take over Sunset Ranch or make a mockery of the Slade family. The other thing he knew would have to wait. He could deal with only one thing right now: finding Sophia. Making sure she was safe.

"Call security and have them comb the area for her. Call me back on my cell if you hear anything."

Logan rose from his desk, his breathing rapid and his strides long and efficient. He made it to Luke's room on the other side of the house in seconds. Pushing open the door, he found Luke still in bed. Alone. Relief registered that he hadn't been wrong about his brother's relationship with Sophia. He wouldn't have to beat the stuffing out of him.

"Logan, man…don't you believe in knocking?"

"Sophia missed a meeting with the staff today. No one's seen her all morning. She's not answering her cell phone. When's the last time you saw her?"

Luke came out of his haze. Since his accident, he'd been sleeping longer than usual in the mornings, making up for uncomfortable nights. "Uh, about nine last night. I checked out her place after dinner and then came home."

"Stay here and make some calls. See what you can find out. I'm going to the cottage."

Still hazy, Luke sat up straighter in the bed, running a hand through his hair. "Will do. Find her, Logan."

"Planning on it."

Logan fired up the truck's engine and sped down the road. Half a mile never seemed so long a drive. He arrived at the cottage and saw that Sophia's car was parked outside. Hope pulled through his fear and he bounded out of the truck, not bothering to knock on the door. He inserted the key he'd kept with him and pushed through the door. "Sophia? Sophia?"

Clearly, she wasn't in the parlor or kitchen. With stealthy steps, Logan moved down the short hallway, wishing he'd taken his gun on the way out. He'd never had cause to use it on the ranch except once when a snake spooked his horse while on a perimeter ride along the property. He'd been thrown within three feet of the irritated rattler. Damn thing had been ready to attack and Logan took aim and shot him dead with that Glock.

Logan didn't know what to make of Sophia's disappearance. She wasn't in the house, but her clothes were still hanging in the closet and her car was parked outside. When he put a hand to the coffeepot, it was lukewarm. She'd used it this morning.

After scanning the kitchen area he searched the parlor. Something caught his eye. He'd almost missed it because the sole thin-stemmed purple wildflower blended in so well with the floral cushions of the sofa. He didn't think much of it. Sophia liked flowers, but as he picked it up and moved pillows around searching for clues, he found something tucked under one square pillow that made his breath catch in his throat.

A note.

Typed on plain paper and folded neatly.

You are very beautiful.

"Son of a bitch!" Logan's mind raced. He'd hoped to high heaven that Sophia's disappearance had been something innocent, a miscommunication that could be cleared up and explained easily enough. He'd hoped she would come waltzing through that front door and find him standing there, worried sick over her.

He took his hat off and stared at the tan leather band, plaguing his mind for a clue. For guidance. The sheriff should be alerted, although the law wouldn't put much credence in a report of a missing woman who'd been gone only an hour. Still, he'd make the call. He'd do anything to make sure Sophia was safe.

Before he could punch the buttons, his cell phone buzzed. He answered his brother's call before it rang again. "Did you find her?"

"Not exactly," Luke said. "Constance said Edward is missing, too. He took Blackie for a walk an hour ago and hasn't returned. He missed his school bus."

"Okay, could be a coincidence. The boy could have lost track of time. Constance have any idea where he might have gone?"

"He likes to walk the dog up by the stream over by the old feed shed. She's mighty worried, Logan."

"I'm on it. I'll check it out and call you—"

Logan stopped midsentence. An unmistakable black-and-white blur raced past the cottage. Logan pushed through the front door and shouted for the dog. "Blackie!"

The dog stopped when he saw him and trotted over with his tail down, completely out of breath. Logan knelt to his level. "Where you going, boy? To the lodge? Where's Edward? Does he need help?"

The dog turned his head in the direction he'd just come from. It didn't take a detective to figure out that Blackie was looking for help. Logan grabbed the dog in his arms and deposited him in the cab of the truck as he finished his conversation with Luke.

"I'm not that far away from the stream. I'm heading there now. I've got the dog. Hopefully, he can lead me to both of them."

Logan drove the truck off-road for three quarters of a mile over gopher holes and rough pasture lands that had been played out. He was headed to the old feed shack that faced a rocky stream that flowed into a pond. It was a perfect place for a young boy to play. Logan and his brothers used to go there after school to look for worms and water snakes.

When he spotted the shed, Logan shut down the engine and parked. He opened the door and the dog scurried over his lap and bounded from the cab racing toward the stream. Logan followed him.

Sophia came into his line of vision first. She sat on a big granite boulder, her leg elevated and her right shoe off. Something squeezed tight in Logan's heart. He shook with profound relief. He'd never been so glad to see anyone in his life. He'd never experienced the kind of fear that threatened to swallow a man up whole and spit him out in small chunks. He'd never been so sure of anything in his life now, looking at Sophia Montrose and realizing that he'd almost let her slip through his fingers.

Edward approached him, his head downcast, a guilty look on his face.

"What happened, Edward?" he asked, still moving toward the boulder where Sophia sat immobilized.

"Ms. Sophia t-twisted her foot. She c-can't walk."

Logan made eye contact with Sophia. Her hair was a mess, her blouse was hanging loose around her skirt and her ankle was twice the size it should be. Raw deep emotion lodged in his throat.

"Why are you out here?" he asked the boy.

Edward shoved his head down again.

"It's okay, Edward. Tell Logan about the notes," Sophia said.

Logan blinked and his voice came out gruff and demanding. "Yeah, tell me about the notes."

Edward stared at the ground. "I t-typed them t-to Ms. Sophia."

Logan's deep voice rose from his throat like a big boom. *"You did what?"*

Edward's body visibly shook.

"It's okay, Logan," Sophia rushed out, putting silent warning in her tone. "Edward explained it to me. He wasn't trying to scare me. Just the opposite. He was feeling a little shy about wanting to be my friend. We've had a long talk this morning. I put two and two together today when I found another note along with the same purple wildflowers that he'd given his grandmother once. I decided to follow Edward out here so we could talk. But I didn't expect to step into a gopher hole and twist my foot along the way."

"Your grandmother is worried sick." Logan tamped down his fury at the boy. It was clear that Sophia wanted to go easy on Edward. Her expression called for mercy and Logan would take heed. Even youngsters like Edward were smitten with Sophia. The rich old coot had it right.

It was hard not to love Sophia.

He was about to call Luke when his brother's Chevy Silverado pulled up next to his truck. Luke and Constance got out and Constance ran over to Edward. The boy was nearly squeezed to death with a big grandmotherly hug. Edward gave her his explanation of what had happened and how he'd sent Blackie for help because he didn't want to leave Sophia alone.

"Luke, take the boy and Constance back to the ranch, will you?" Logan said after all the apologies were made. Sophia made sure Edward's actions were painted in a better light than he deserved, in Logan's opinion. And Constance was happy enough to have her grandson back safely. She promised to make sure Edward understood the consequences of what he'd done. Logan thought the boy skated, but his concern now was for Sophia. "And call off the search."

"Will do." Luke glanced at Sophia's injured foot and took a step toward her.

"Luke." Logan gave his brother a firm warning. "I've got this."

Luke's gaze darted to Sophia. She sat regally on that boulder, doing a good job of concealing her physical pain with her arms crossed over her body and displeasure curling her mouth. "Sure thing, bro. You just let me know how that works out for you."

Logan waited for Luke's engine to roar to life, and the three of them were well on the road before he walked over to Sophia. She eyed him suspiciously and flinched a little when he leaned close to inspect her injured leg. He took it as a good sign that he still made her nervous and at this point; he'd take any crumb she offered.

He pushed his hat back on his head and lifted her ankle gently.

"Ow!"

"Did you hear a snap when you stepped in that gopher hole?" he asked.

"No."

"Probably just sprained, then."

She looked away. "Great."

Logan finished his inspection of her leg and set it down with care.

"You were too easy on the boy."

"It wasn't his fault. He honestly had no idea that I'd be frightened by the notes he sent. He's a shy boy who's had a rough life and I think he wanted us to be friends."

"The boy is smitten with you." He rubbed the back of his neck and sighed. "I get that. You have that effect on most men."

"That's not true."

She was being argumentative, and considering that he was her ride back to the ranch, Logan had to give her credit for her feisty attitude. "Let's say that you're right and I'm wrong."

"I am right," she said with a curt nod as if the subject was closed.

Logan sat his butt down next to her on the boulder. He stretched out his long legs, his boots digging into the earth. The soft purr of the lazy stream flowing by and a few birds flitting from tree to tree filled the silence. "Okay, then it's just me who thinks you're a beautiful, smart, kindhearted, hardworking woman with a body that makes me want to cry, and those big—"

"Logan!"

Logan chuckled and the movement knocked his shoulder against hers. "Eyes, Sophia. I was going to say big eyes."

Sophia didn't crack a smile. Her face crumpled with confusion. "You're not making any sense. You don't think those things about me. You've let me know exactly what you think of me, and it doesn't bear repeating."

"I know I was scared half out of my mind when I thought you were missing. Horrible thoughts entered my head of a stalker getting to you. I was going a little crazy until I pulled up and saw you on this boulder. I know I wouldn't have survived if anything had happened to you. I was wrong about you, Sophia."

"You were cruel to me. Those things you said."

"I didn't know you were listening. I said those things to Luke, because…I've always been a little jealous of your friendship. And I knew then what I was afraid to admit to myself up until today. I love you, Sophia. I love you so much, it scares me silly."

Sophia's ankle throbbed and she thought for certain the pain had gone to her head. She was sure she was hearing things. "You *love* me?"

"I've never said those words to a woman before. I've never wanted to. I've never believed in true love. Until now."

"So you don't believe all those awful things about me?"

"If you explain it to me, I'm ready to listen. I'll believe you, no matter what."

Sophia didn't hesitate. She'd wanted to clear the air for a long time. She'd wanted Logan to hear the truth and really have him hear her. "I didn't marry Gordon for his money, you have to know that. He was a friend and I needed his help."

Sophia spent the next few minutes explaining about Gordon Gregory and his granddaughter Amanda. She told Logan about the friendship that had developed afterward and how Gordon had offered to help both Louisa and Sophia when they'd had nowhere else to turn.

"I didn't ask for anything else from Gordon. And I never slept with him, Logan. I never did. That's why we divorced. After my mother passed, he put pressure on me. He claims he fell in love with me, but I didn't love him. I never felt that way about him." She repeated, "I never slept with him."

"But you slept with me."

Sophia closed her eyes briefly, taking a leap of faith again because there was nothing left for her to lose. Because everything she wanted was right here in front of her. She placed her faith and trust in Logan one last time. "Yes, I slept with you. I fell in love. Don't ask me why, Logan. I have no idea why I love you. By all rights I should have fallen in love with

Luke. But I don't feel that way about your brother. He and I are friends. Period."

Logan turned his body to fully face Sophia. She saw a look in his eyes, the same look Randall Slade had for her mother. The same look that every woman deserved to see in the eyes of the man she loved. "You love me?"

She nodded.

His lips rose in a quick smile and he took her hand, applying sweet pressure. He spoke in a voice steeped with determination. "I don't want our love to go to waste, Sophia. Not the way our parents' did. I can't deny what I feel for you anymore. Ever since that kiss in high school, I think I've always known there was something special between us. Something undeniable."

"I felt it, too," she whispered. "And I don't want our love to go to waste, either."

"Forgive me for being hard on you. I was a fool."

Hearing Logan admit his past mistakes and ask for her forgiveness was an intoxicating gift from the man she loved. "I think I can forgive you."

Logan's arms came around her. Gently he lifted her from the rock and cradled her, taking care with her swollen ankle. He brought his mouth ever so close. "Kiss me, Sophia."

She smiled. "You won't think I'm easy?"

"Nothing about you and me is easy, sweetheart."

She brought her mouth close and brushed her lips over his softly. Tension released from his body, his stance no longer rigidly defensive. The walls of mistrust and suspicion he'd built to protect himself came tumbling down around her until what remained was the rightness of their love.

It was Logan's ultimate surrender.

The battle was over. The kiss they shared was their beacon, a bright glow of light guiding their way out of the darkness. He loved her and she loved him. It had been complicated

between them for most of their lives. But now it was just…
simple.

"I love you, Logan Slade."

He kissed her tenderly and when he spoke his voice was
husky and rich with reverence. "Marry me, Sophia. Live with
me on Sunset Ranch. Be my partner, my friend, my wife."

Sophia set her palm on the sharp handsome plane of his
cheekbone and gazed deeply into his eyes. "I was never any
of those things before, but I want to be everything to you now.
Yes, Logan. I'll marry you."

Logan smiled, love shining in his eyes. "I'm a lucky man."

"And I'm a happy woman."

He took off his Stetson and in one smooth move, placed it
on her head, giving it a tug to secure the fit. "I can't wait to
make you a Slade. My father always said you were a woman
who'd make a fine wife."

They were words Sophia never thought she'd hear from
Logan.

"Do you think your father set this up?"

Logan contemplated for a moment. "From his grave?"

"No, but maybe before he died? I could never figure out
why he was so generous with me in his will. Do you think
he wanted me to find love on Sunset Ranch?"

Logan gave the notion some thought. "It's possible. My dad
loved you like a daughter and, Lord above, everyone knew
how much he loved the ranch."

Sophia's eyes misted with tears. "And his boys. He loved
his sons, Logan. Don't forget that."

Logan nodded and clear understanding filled his eyes.
"Maybe it was his secret wish that you marry a Slade, sweetheart."

"It would be nice to think so. Can you ever forgive your
father, Logan?"

"If he brought you to me I can surely forgive him."

Sophia smiled and he wiped a tear from her cheek. "Then let's just believe it as truth."

"I can do that."

Something good and long-lasting would come from Randall's love for Louisa.

And perhaps their love hadn't been wasted after all.

Sophia clung to that notion as hard and as tight as she held on to her cowboy.

With Logan's love surrounding her, she could finally call Sunset Ranch…home.

* * * * *

#2209 THE KING NEXT DOOR

Kings of California

Maureen Child

Griffin King has strict rules about getting involved with a single mother, but temptation is right next door.

#2210 BEDROOM DIPLOMACY

Daughters of Power: The Capital

Michelle Celmer

A senator's daughter ends up as a bargaining chip that could divert a besotted diplomat's attention to marriage negotiations instead!

#2211 A REAL COWBOY

Rich, Rugged Ranchers

Sarah M. Anderson

He's given up Hollywood for his ranch and doesn't want to go back. How far will she go to sign him to the role of a lifetime?

#2212 MARRIAGE WITH BENEFITS

Winner of Harlequin's 2011 SYTYCW contest

Kat Cantrell

Cia Allende needs a husband—so she can divorce him and gain her trust fund. She doesn't expect that the man she's handpicked will become someone she can't live without.

#2213 ALL HE REALLY NEEDS

At Cain's Command

Emily McKay

When lovers must suddenly work together to unravel a mystery from his family's past, their private affair threatens to become very public.

#2214 A TRICKY PROPOSITION

Cat Schield

When Ming asks her best friend to help her become a mother, he persuades her to conceive the old-fashioned way. But will his brother—Ming's ex-fiancé—stand in the way?

HDI3

Rediscover the Harlequin series section starting December 18!

NEW LOOK
....
ON SALE DECEMBER 18

Lying in Bed

The Other Side of Us

LONGER BOOK, NEW LOOK
....
ON SALE DECEMBER 18

LONGER BOOK, NEW LOOK
....
ON SALE DECEMBER 18

HEATHER GRAHAM
KEEPER OF THE NIGHT

COWBOY WITH A CAUSE
Carla Cassidy

LONGER BOOK, NEW LOOK
....
ON SALE DECEMBER 18

THE ONE THAT GOT AWAY
KELLY HUNTER

NEW SERIES HARLEQUIN KISS™!
....
ON SALE JANUARY 22

SPECIAL EXCERPT FROM HARLEQUIN® KISS™

Evangeline is surprised when her past lover turns out to be her fiancé's brother. How will she manage the one she loved and the one she has made a deal with?

Follow her path to love January 22, 2013, with

THE ONE THAT GOT AWAY

by Kelly Hunter

"The trouble with memories like ours," he said roughly, "is that you think you've buried them, dealt with them, right up until they reach up and rip out your throat."

Some memories were like that. But not all. Sometimes memories could be finessed into something slightly more palatable.

"Maybe we could try replacing the bad with something a little less intense," she suggested tentatively. "You could try treating me as your future sister-in-law. We could do polite and civil. We could come to like it that way."

"Watching you hang off my brother's arm doesn't make me feel civilized, Evangeline. It makes me want to break things."

Ah.

"Call off the engagement." He wasn't looking at her. And it wasn't a request. "Turn this mess around."

"We need Max's trust fund money."

"I'll cover Max for the money. I'll buy you out."

"What?" Anger slid through her, hot and biting. She could feel her composure slipping away but there was nothing else for it. Not in the face of the hot mess that was Logan. "No," she said as steadily as she could. "No one's buying me out of anything, least of all MEP. That company is *mine,* just as much as it is Max's. I've put six years into it, eighty-hour weeks of blood, sweat, tears and fears into making it the success it is. Prepping it for bigger opportunities, and one of those opportunities is just around the corner. Why on earth would I let you buy me out?"

He meant to use his big body to intimidate her. Closer, and closer still, until the jacket of his suit brushed the silk of her dress, but he didn't touch her, just let the heat build. His lips had that hard sensual curve about them that had haunted her dreams for years. She couldn't stop staring at them.

She needed to stop staring at them.

"You can't be in my life, Lena. Not even on the periphery. I discovered that the hard way ten years ago. So either you leave willingly…or I make you leave."

Find out what Evangeline decides to do by picking up THE ONE THAT GOT AWAY by Kelly Hunter. Available January 22, 2013, wherever Harlequin books are sold.